HOME of the BRAVE

Katherine Applegate

FEIWEL AND FRIENDS
New York

A FEIWEL AND FRIENDS BOOK
An Imprint of Holtzbrinck Publishers

The author and publisher gratefully acknowledge Ahmed Elmi, Refugee Services, Refugee & Employment Programs, Lutheran Social Services of Minnesota, for his expert review of this work.

Library of Congress Cataloging-in-Publication Data

Applegate, Katherine.
    Home of the brave / Katherine Applegate.
        p. cm.
    Summary: Kek, an African refugee, is confronted by many strange things at the Minneapolis home of his aunt and cousin, as well as in his fifth-grade classroom, and longs for his missing mother, but finds comfort in the company of a cow and her owner.
    ISBN:13 978-0-312-36765-7 / ISBN:10 0-312-36765-1
    [1. Immigrants—Fiction. 2. African Americans—Fiction. 3. Schools—Fiction. 4. Cows—Fiction. 5. Hope—Fiction. 6. Minneapolis (Minn.)—Fiction.] I. Title.
PZ7.A6485Hom 2007
[Fic]—dc22

                                                                                            2006032053

First Edition: September 2007

10 9 8 7 6 5 4 3 2 1

Book design by Kristina Albertson

For Michael, Jake, and Julia, with love

PART ONE

When elephants fight, it is
the grass that suffers.
—AFRICAN PROVERB

SNOW

When the flying boat
returns to earth at last,
I open my eyes
and gaze out the round window.
What is all the white? I whisper.
Where is all the world?

The helping man greets me
and there are many lines and questions
and pieces of paper.

At last I follow him outside.
We call that snow, he says.
Isn't it beautiful?
Do you like the cold?

I want to say
No, this cold is like claws on my skin!

I look around me.
Dead grass pokes through
the unkind blanket of white.
Everywhere the snow
sparkles with light
hard as high sun.
I close my eyes.
I try out my new English words:
How can you live
in this place called America?
It burns your eyes!

The man gives me a fat shirt
and soft things like hands.
Coat, he says. Gloves.
He smiles. You'll get used to it, Kek.

I am a tall boy,
like all my people.
My arms stick out of the coat
like lonely trees.
My fingers cannot make
the gloves work.

I shake my head.
I say, This America is hard work.

His laughter makes little clouds.

OLD WORDS, NEW WORDS

The helping man
is called Dave.
He tells me he's from the
Refugee Resettlement Center,
but I don't know what those
words are trying to say.

He isn't tall
like my father was,
and there is hair on his face
the color of clouds before rain.
His car is red
and coughs and burps
when he tries to make it go.
Doesn't much like
the cold, either, he says.

I smile to say I understand,
although I do not.

Sometimes Dave speaks English,
the tangled sounds

they tried to teach us
in the refugee camp.
And sometimes he
uses my words.
He's like a song always out of tune,
missing notes.

To help him,
I try some English,
but my mouth just wants to chew the words
and spit them on the ground.

We are like a cow and a goat,
wanting to be friends
but wondering if it
can ever be.

QUESTIONS

We drive past buildings,
everywhere buildings.
Everywhere cars.
Everywhere dead trees.
Who killed all the trees? I ask.

They're not dead, Dave says.
This is called winter,
and it happens every year.
In spring their leaves will come back.
You'll see.

He turns to smile.
His eyes are wise and calm,
the eyes of a village elder.
Your family will be happy
to see you, Dave says,
but he doesn't mean my truest family,
my mother and father and brother.

I don't answer.
I reach into my pocket

and feel the soft cloth
I carry with me everywhere.
Blue and yellow,
torn at the edges,
the size of my hand,
soft as new grass after good rain.

Dave asks, When did you last see
your aunt and cousin?

A long time ago, I say.
Before the camp.

I can tell that Dave
has many questions.
I wonder if all America people
will be so curious.
My mouth is going to get very sore,
stumbling on words all day long.

We stop at a light
hung high in the air,
red and round
like a baby sun.
How was the airplane trip?

Dave asks in English.
When I don't answer, he tries again,
using my words:
Did you like the flying boat?

I liked it very much, I say.
I'd like to fly such a boat
one day myself.
When Mama comes,
we'll take a flying boat
around the world.

Dave turns to look at me.
You know, Kek, he says,
we aren't sure where your mother is.
His voice has the soft sting of pity in it.
We don't know if she is—

She's fine, I tell him,
and I look out the window
at the not-dead trees.
She will come, I say,
and this time
I use my words,
my music.

WHAT THE HECK

We drive down a long road
with many fast cars.
Still there are buildings,
but sometimes not.
I see a long fence
made of old gray boards.
And then I see the cow.

Stop! I yell.
I feel regret in my heart
to use such a harsh sound
with my new helping friend.
Please stop, I say,
gently this time.

What? Dave asks.
What's wrong?

Did you not see her?
The brave cow
in the snow?

Dave glances
in the looking-back glass.
Cow? Oh, yeah. That used to be
a big farm. Lot of land around here's
getting sold off now.
But that farmer's hanging on.

I don't understand his words,
but I can hear that he doesn't
love cattle as I do,
and I feel sorry for him.
I twist in my seat.
The don't-move belt across my chest
pulls back.

Oh, what the heck? Dave says.

I have not yet learned
the meaning of *heck,*
but I can see that
it's a fine and useful word,
because he turns the car around.

GOD WITH A WET NOSE

We park by the side
of the fast-car road.
Walking through the snow
is hard work,
like wading across a river
wild with rain.

The cow is near a fine,
wide-armed,
good-for-climbing tree.
To say the truth of it,
she is not the most beautiful of cows.
Her belly sags
and her coat is scarred
and her face tells me
she remembers sweeter days.

My father would not have stood
for such a weary old woman in his herd,
and yet to see her here
in this strange land
makes my eyes glad.

In my old home back in Africa,
cattle mean life.
They are our reason
to rise with the sun,
to move with the rains,
to rest with the stars.
They are the way we know
our place in the world.

The cow looks past me.
I can see that she's pouting,
with only snow and dead grass
to keep her company.

I shake my head. A cow can be trouble,
with her slow, stubborn body,
her belly ripe with milk,
her pleading eyes that shine at you
like river rocks in sun.

An old woman comes out of the barn.
She's carrying a bucket.
Two chickens trot behind her
scolding and fussing.
The woman waves.

Just saying hello to the cow,
Dave calls.

Let me know if she answers,
the woman calls back,
and she returns to the barn.

We should go, Dave says.
Your aunt is expecting us.

A little longer, I say.
Please?

I know cattle are important
to your people, Dave says.
Again he tries to use my words.
A man I helped to settle here
taught me a saying from Africa.
I'll bet you would like it:
A cow is God with a wet nose.

I laugh. We wait.
The wind sneaks through my coat.
My teeth shiver.
I take off a glove

and hold out my hand,
and at last the cow comes to me.

She moos,
a harsh and mournful sound.
It isn't the fault of the cow.
She doesn't know another way to talk.
She can't learn
the way I am learning,
word
by slow, slow
word.

I stroke her cold, wet coat,
and for a moment I hold
all I've lost
and all I want
right there in my hand.

WELCOME TO MINNESOTA

It's growing dark
when I say good-bye to the cow
and we go back to the car to drive again.
At last we park before a brown building,
taller than trees.
Its window-eyes
weep yellow light.

Under a street lamp,
children throw white balls
at the not-dead trees.
Snowballs, Dave explains.
A smiling girl throws
one of the balls at Dave's car.
He shakes his head.
Welcome to Minnesota, he says.

We climb out of the car.
The snowball girl's face is red
and her long brown hair is wet.
Hi, she says. I'm Hannah.
You the new kid?

I'm not sure of the answer,
so I make my shoulders go up and down.
Catch, she says,
and she throws a cold white ball to me.
It falls apart in my hands.

I follow Dave across the noisy snow.
Two times I slip and fall.
Two times I rise, pants wet, knees burning.

Take it slow, buddy, Dave says.

Tears trace my cheeks like tiny knives.
I look away so Dave will not see my shame.
How can I trust a place
where even the ground plays tricks?

Inside, we climb up many stairs.
We walk down a long hall,
passing door after door.
Dave knocks on one of them,
and behind it I hear the
muffled voices of my past.

Much time has come and gone,
but still I know the worn, gray voice
of my mother's sister, Nyatal.
I hear another voice, too,
the sound of a young man,
a strong man.

The door opens
and my old life is waiting on the other side.

FAMILY

I'm hugged and kissed
and there is much welcoming
from my aunt.
She's rounder than I remember,
with a moon face to match,
her black eyes set deep.

My cousin, Ganwar,
shakes my hand.
I have learned about shaking hands.
At the camp they taught us how:
be firm, but do not squeeze too hard!
Still, when Ganwar grasps my hand
we are like two calves in the clouds
pretending we know how to fly.

The man's voice belongs to Ganwar,
and he has my father's height now,
though Ganwar is thin and reedy
where my father
was sturdy with strength.
His eyes are wary and smart,

always taking the measure of a person.
Six long scars line his forehead,
the marks of manhood
I watched Ganwar and my brother receive
in our village ceremony.
How jealous I had been that day,
too young for such an honor.

I try hard not to look at
another scar,
the place where Ganwar's left hand
should be,
round and bare and waiting
like an ugly question
no one can answer.

The night Ganwar lost his hand
was the night I lost
my father and brother,
the night of men in the sky with guns,
the night the earth opened up like a black pit
and swallowed my old life whole.

My aunt holds my face in her hands
and I see that she's crying.

I know her to be a woman of many sorrows,
carved down to a sharp stone
by her luckless life.
She isn't like my mother,
whose laughter is
like bubbling water from a deep spring.

I look into her eyes
and then my tears come hard and fast,
not for her, not for my cousin,
not even for myself,
but because when I look there,
I see my mother's eyes
looking back at me.

LESSONS

I'll let you get settled, Dave says,
but first I'll give you some lessons.
Your aunt and your cousin know these things,
but you'll need to know them, too.

Number one, he says,
always lock your door.
Ganwar, show Kek what a key looks like.

In my old home,
my real home,
my father kept us safe.
We had no need for locks.

Number two, he says,
this is a light switch.
He pushes a tiny stick on the wall
and the room turns to night,
then blinks awake.

In my old home,
my real home,

the sun gave us light,
and the stars
watched us sleep.

This thermostat, Dave says,
helps keep you warm.
He pretends to shiver
to paint a picture for his words.

In my old home,
my real home,
we were a family,
and our laughter kept us warm.
We didn't need a magic switch
on a wall.

I nod to say yes,
I understand,
but I wonder if I will ever understand,
even if Dave stands here,
pointing and talking
forever.

GOOD-BYES

I'll be going now, Kek, Dave says,
but I'll see you tomorrow.
I smile to show my thanking.

Remember that this'll take time, he says.
It isn't easy to make such a big change.
Things are very different here.

In the camp, I say,
they called America
heaven on earth.

They say many things in the camps, Ganwar says.
You'll see how wrong they were.

Dave shakes his finger at Ganwar.
You behaving lately, buddy?
he asks with a smile.

My aunt answers
when Ganwar doesn't:
He had another fight last week.

Ganwar looks at the ceiling.
At least I won.

I'll talk to your counselor at school, Dave says.
I wonder from his sound if he has said
these words before.

Ganwar and I will go to school together?
I ask with hope.

No, Dave says.
Ganwar is in eleventh grade,
and you will be in fifth.
He pats my back.
Kek, if you need anything,
have your aunt get in touch with me.
I'm always here to help.

I will be OK, I say,
using my best English words.
Soon I will make snowballs.

I make a big grin
so that my new friend Dave
will not worry.

I wonder if he can tell
it is a pretending smile.

Kek, my aunt says,
he's a good boy.
He will try hard
to make his new life work.

I can hear her struggle to
find the English words,
just like I do.

My aunt glances at Ganwar.
You'll see, Dave.
Kek finds sun
when the sky is dark.

Ah, says Dave,
an optimist.

I look away.
I cannot find any sun today, I think.

Dave shakes my hand,
and when the door closes behind him

I'm surprised that I feel afraid,
a little bit.

Dave isn't like my father,
not at all.
But it's been good
to have someone watching over me,
even for just a while.
It's been a long time
since I've known that feeling,
like a soft blanket
on a night when the wind howls.

FATHER

He had many cattle,
my father,
and the respect of our village,
but it was his voice that made him
a rich man among men.
His voice was deep,
like a storm coming,
but gentle,
like the rain ending.

My people are herders.
We move with the seasons,
with the wet and the dry,
so that the cattle
may be strong and well fed.
We cannot carry much with us,
and so our stories don't
make their homes
in heavy books.
We hold our stories
in our songs.

No one knew more songs
than my father,
and no one sang them
with a voice as clear and sure.

He knew songs of the stars
and the wind,
of love and betrayal,
of war and regret.
Always the villagers would beg,
just one more song, Dak!
Our ears long for one more story!

At night, before we went to sleep,
my father would make new songs
for my brother Lual and me.
He sang my favorite
the night he was killed:

The crocodile snaps;
Still Kek swims.

The feet bleed;
Still Kek dances.

The calf vanishes;
Still Kek searches.

The sandstorm blinds;
Still Kek laughs.

My stubborn Kek,
my willful son,
if you tell me
you can dance with the wind,
if you tell me
you can sleep with the lion,
if you tell me
you can harvest the stars,
how can I doubt you,
my son?

BED

We must feed you.
My aunt speaks in my language,
the right way,
with the notes where they belong.
Ganwar will show you the other rooms.

There are more? I ask.
How can that be?
You have a kingdom here!
A TV machine, a sitting place,
a cooking fire!

The smile on Ganwar's face
is a surprise.
Suddenly I remember him
playing with my brother,
wild boys chasing each other like
lion and prey,
searching out mischief
in every corner of our village.

Ganwar leads me to a little room.
For bathing, he instructs.
But watch out.
The water comes hot and fast.

I point to the magic water pot
like the one on the flying boat.
You don't go outside?

He laughs. It would turn to yellow ice.

I laugh, too.
Ganwar stares at me.
Always his eyes seem to know
more than I will ever know.

You laugh like your brother, he says.
He is quiet. His grin is gone.

Too bad I do not look like him, I say,
and I am glad to see Ganwar's smile return.
It means we will not talk of
why I am here
and Lual is not.

Too bad for sure,
Ganwar agrees.

I have a silly face, to tell the truth of it.
I have the eyelashes of a girl,
as Lual and Ganwar liked to remind me.
My ears look like they want
to fly me away,
and my smile takes up most of my face.

My brother was the handsome one.
Everywhere girls watched him
with shy, smiling eyes.

Another room is waiting.
On the floor
lie blankets and pillows
like gentle dunes.
I run my hands over covers
softer than a new calf 's coat.
Just one mattress so far,
says Ganwar,
and his voice tells me this is not a good thing.
Dave says maybe he can find more soon.

You and I will sleep in the other room.
We'll take turns on the sofa.

So-fa? I repeat.

It's a long chair
you can sleep on, Ganwar explains.

You don't need to share, I say.
I'll try not to get in the way.

You know you are welcome here, Ganwar says,
but I cannot tell if he means his words.

It's a strange pain
to be with those you belong to
and feel you don't belong.

Carefully I take a step
onto the blanket cloud.
I stumble, then stand,
then jump and jump
and fall
and jump some more.

Ganwar shakes his head.
You haven't changed,
my cousin, he says.
You're still a crazy little boy.

I stop my jumping.
I'm not a little boy, I think.
Not anymore.
But I keep the words in my heart.

BROTHER

My brother Lual was Ganwar's age,
and just as tall.
Maybe that's why he tried
always to tell me what to do.
Have you lost your ears,
my stubborn brother? he would say.
You must listen to our father and mother.
Soon you'll be a man,
not a silly boy.

I would sigh,
I would laugh,
and once I even slipped
two snakes onto his sleeping mat
while he lay snoring.
The whole village awoke to his screams.
I know it was wrong to do,
but they were harmless snakes,
and when I saw Lual's face
I laughed until
my eyes rained.

Every day Lual scolded,
and every day I thought,
Lual, please just be my brother.
I don't need two fathers!

I didn't know that too soon
I would not have any.

Still, though he could peck at me
like a sharp-beaked bird,
Lual knew well how to make
his little brother laugh.
He would have known a soft bed
was made for jumping.
He would have growled at me
for misbehaving,
but then,
when no one was looking,
he would have jumped just as high.

I would give all the beds
in all the great world
to feel the sharp thorn
of Lual's scolding once again.

TV MACHINE

My aunt makes food on the cooking fire.
We eat simply,
with tastes and smells of my home,
and we talk with the words and sounds I know
sweet in my mouth.

But the more home returns to me,
the more I remember all I've lost.
I feel the holes where
my mother,
my father,
my brother
should be,
my uncle, my aunt's husband,
and their other children, too—
two girls, younger than Ganwar.

Sometimes, it seems to me,
a hole can be
as real and solid
as a boulder or a tree.

Outside snowflakes tap at the window
like stubborn mosquitoes.
I try out the word—
snow—
then shiver and shake
just like Dave.

My aunt lets a smile go free.
I have to go to work now, she says.

What do you mean, work? I want to know.

Mama helps at a house for old people, Ganwar explains.
His mouth is a line.
It's not a good place.

It's called a nursing home, says my aunt.
And they pay me money
so that I can buy things.
It takes a lot of money to live here in America.

But it's night, I say.
And it's cold.

My aunt touches my shoulder.
You're a good boy, Kek.
You are your mother's child.

Mama will be glad to see you, I say.
I hope she'll get here soon.

My aunt looks at me with
questions in her eyes.
She glances at Ganwar.
He looks away.

Don't hope too hard,
she says in a whispering voice,
and then she puts on her coat and leaves.

When she's gone,
Ganwar and I watch the TV machine.
I'd seen one at the airport
and on the flying boat,
but this machine has
many more stories,
more colors,
more happy people

and mad people.
People are dancing
and singing
and shooting
and kissing.
So many people,
but they still cannot fill
the holes in the room.

NIGHT

The pillow like a mound of grass
under my head is good comfort,
and the blanket is warm as afternoon sun,
but still I can't sleep.

Ganwar lies without moving,
but I know somehow
he is not sleeping, either.

After a while Ganwar sits up on his elbows.
He's just a shadow to my eyes.
What's that cloth you're holding? he asks.

It's from the camp, I say.
It's true,
true enough.
I don't want to say
the whole truth.

Are you glad that you're here, Ganwar?
I ask.

He breathes in and out, in and out.

This is a good land, he says.
There's great freedom here.
But even when you travel far,
the ghosts don't stay behind.
They follow you.
You come here to make a new life,
but the old life is still haunting you.

We don't say anything for a few minutes.
Finally Ganwar speaks.
They're all gone, Kek.
They're all dead.

I want to hate Ganwar for his words.
But I am too weary for anger.
Already there are so many people to hate,
too many.

Not all, I finally whisper.
Not Mama.

He sighs. It isn't good to fool yourself.
I've learned that much.

Hoping isn't foolish, I say.
If I can make it all the way here,
then anything can happen.
He shakes his head.
Crazy boy, Ganwar says.
Hoping doesn't make a thing true.
Remember when you were
no taller than my knee
and you thought you
could talk to the cattle?

They listened, I say.
They just didn't answer.

How about when you
believed you could fly?
Remember how you jumped from the top
of the acacia tree?

I still have the scar on my elbow, I say.
And anyway, the flying part was fun.
Only the landing was troublesome.

You can't make yourself a bird, Kek.
Some things will never be.

A man does not give up, I say.

A man knows when he's defeated, Ganwar replies.

I wipe away a tear
with the soft cloth in my hand.

I don't answer.
I am afraid of what the answer might be.

MAMA

I have my father's will,
my brother's eyes,
and my mother's light.

She is like newborn sun,
fresh with promise,
the just-beginning moments
before the day
fills like a bucket
with good and bad,
sweat and longing.

Even her laughter has sun in it.

Always when I think of her
I see a cloudless day blooming full,
I feel warmth on my shoulders,
I know hope's embrace.

I am just a boy like any boy.
I make trouble,
I'm lazy,

I kick at the world
when I'm mad.

I don't know why I have been so lucky,
to be so loved.

SLEEP STORY

I am on the flying boat
and so is Dave and
Mama and Father and Lual.
People from my village
are there, and many cows,
and a camel and a gazelle.
Airplane, Dave says,
Try to say it, Kek.
But when my mouth opens,
the only things that come out
are little white puffs,
cloud after cloud.
You must try harder,
Lual says,
and I give him my best scowl.
He laughs, and then
the round windows open
and guns are there
and hating words,
and I am screaming
empty white clouds of fear.
When at last it's quiet,

the seats of Lual and my father
and all the other men from my village
are empty.
They're gone, I tell my mama,
they're dead,
and she takes my hand.
When we step outside
it isn't sky we see,
but endless, barren land
dotted with dead trees.
Mile after mile
day after day
tear after tear
we travel,
to a place of tents and women and children.
Here in the camp we are safe, she says.
The men with guns will not come.
My feet are blistered
and her dress of blue and yellow
is stained with blood,
and all around us
snow falls
and my eyes burn
with the sight of it.

PART TWO

You only make a bridge
where there is a river.
—AFRICAN PROVERB

PAPERWORK

Dave comes for me the next day.
He has snow in his eyebrows.
We drive in the red rattling car
to a new place.
Refugee Resettlement Center, Dave calls it.

It's warm there,
with many chairs
and many more people,
all colors and shapes.
It's my job to answer
a bored lady's questions.
Her fingers bounce on
a machine with many buttons
while she stares at a bright box.
Her fingernails are shiny red,
the color of blood,

and I feel sorry
for her bad fortune.

At first I'm afraid to speak.
It's OK, Kek, Dave says.
It's called paperwork.
You can't make a wrong answer here.

The bored lady asks her questions again,
and this time I answer.

Soon I grow sleepy,
and after a while her words
begin to fall like raindrops on the floor.
I try to understand,
but all I hear is a river of words,
rushing and thundering
and pushing me beneath the surface.
Now and then a word I know
darts up like a sparkling fish,
but then it's all dark
moving water again.

We are there a long time.
I don't think

I like this America paperwork,
I whisper to Dave.
It makes for
too many yawnings.

INFORMATION

Dave leads me to another room.
A woman sits behind a pile of papers
tall as a termite mound.
Is this Kek, by any chance? she asks Dave.

One and only, he says.
Kek, meet Diane.

Diane stands and shakes my hand.
She isn't much taller than I am,
but her grip is strong
and she meets my gaze
with eyes that say she is a friend.

We've been trying to get more information
on your mom, Kek, Diane says.
Here's what we've got.
She hands many papers to Dave.

My hope flutters high
like a bird I cannot catch.

I ready my heart for the words I need to hear:
Found her. Good news. Coming here.
Those are the words Diane must say.
Those are the stars that will guide my path home.

This is a very difficult process,
I'm afraid, Diane says.
Refugees in that area move frequently,
and tracking someone down can be
almost impossible.
We've sent out an inquiry
about two camps on the border.

Diane pauses.
I wait to hear the words,
to see the stars.

After your camp was attacked,
some people made it to the places we're contacting.
I don't want you to get your hopes up, Kek.
We'll know more in a while.

Diane looks at some papers.
Dave looks at his shoes.

I am still hoping, I say at last.
I want to sound fierce and certain
as a great lion.
But I sound like a lost cub,
even to my own ears.

Of course you are, Diane says.
We all are.

Thank you for your looking, I say.

Diane nods. You're very welcome.
I'll be in touch with Dave as soon as we hear anything.

We head outside.
The icy air kicks at my chest.
We walk to Dave's car in silence.
Only the snow talks.

We climb in.
Seat belt, Dave says softly.
I am glad he doesn't ask how I am feeling.
I don't know whether to feel

hope or fear.
Dave pushes a knob
and the music box sings.
The song races ahead while I stumble behind,
just one more thing I cannot know.

SCHOOL CLOTHES

That night,
I try on the school clothes
in the box Dave has brought for me.
I pick a button shirt with flowers on it
and soft red pants,
but Ganwar rolls his eyes.
Those are pajamas, he says.
You wear them when you sleep.

I try again.
Ganwar shakes his head.
The kids will eat you alive, he says.

This is bad news,
since I didn't know that America people
like to eat each other.
Ganwar must see the fear in my eyes
because he explains:
It means they'll beat you up.

Oh, I say. I feel relieved.
You mean like at the camp?

I'm not much of a fighter,
not like my brother and my father
and my cousin.
I'm used to losing fights.
It isn't so bad,
if you cover your face
and other important places.

Ganwar finds a pair of hard blue pants
and a shirt the color of sand.
Jeans, he says. T-shirt.
I put them on and parade
through the TV room
like a great ruler.

Ganwar groans.
It's just school, Kek.

My aunt hushes him.
Let him have his fun, she scolds.

In the bathing room
I look hard in the shiny glass.
I wonder if I look
like an America boy.

I'm not sure if that would be
a good thing or a not-good thing.

ONCE THERE WAS . . .

The next morning,
I don't know what I am feeling.
I'm excited, yes,
because to go to school and learn
is a fine honor.
But I'm worried also.
I don't know so many things.
I don't even know
what I don't know!
My belly leaps
like a monkey on a tree.

In the camp we had a teacher
some days, yes,
some days, no.
Some days I was too ill
with the fever to go.
Some days the teacher couldn't come
because of the men with guns.

But on the good days,
the teacher might arrive

with a piece of chalk
and maybe even a book.
Mostly he would help us
learn English words,
so we would be ready
to leave the camp someday.

But sometimes there would be
singing, or a story
or numbers on our fingers and toes to count.

I liked the stories the best.
Once there was
a lion who could not roar . . .
Once there was
a man who sailed the sea . . .
Once there was
a child who found a treasure . . .
The stories would lift me up,
the words like a breeze beneath
butterfly wings,
and take me far from the pain in my belly
and the tight knot of my heart.

I hope they will have stories
at my school.
If they don't know how,
perhaps I can teach them.
It isn't such a hard thing.
All you must do is say
Once there was . . .
and then let your hoping find the words.

NEW DESK

Dave takes me to school.
When I see it, I use the words
I learned from the TV machine:
No way!
It's big enough to graze
a herd of cattle in,
made of fine, red square stones
and surrounded by many
tall not-dead trees.
It's a place for
a leader of men to work in,
not a place for small children
to learn their numbers.

Dave sees my falling-open mouth.
Don't be scared, Kek, he says.
But I'm not scared,
not like that.
Scared is for men with guns
and maybe just a little
for a flying boat

finding its way
back to earth.

Inside my school
the floor shines like ice.
I walk carefully.
Thin metal doors with silver handles
line the walls.
Those are called lockers, Dave says.
C'mon. We're early,
but the teacher wants to meet you.

Waiting in a big-windowed room
is a woman with black hair that dances
and sturdy arms
and eyes that tell jokes.
You must be Kek, she says,
and then she uses my word
for hello.

I'm ready to begin
my learning, I say,
and she tosses out a loud laugh
like a ball into the air.

I can see you mean business, she says.
A man comes in,
young and short
with skin the color of rich earth,
just like mine.
He says he is Mr. Franklin
and he helps sometimes in class
when Ms. Hernandez needs
to do her deep breathing.
Everyone laughs,
so I laugh, too,
because it's always
good to be polite.

This will be your desk, Ms. Hernandez says.
Have a seat.
She points to a shiny chair
and little table.

A chair of my own
and a table, too?
I smother the thought
like an ember near dry grass.

I'm very sorry, but I can't,
I say softly. I don't have the cattle
for such a fine desk as this.

Oh, she says,
you don't have to pay for this desk, Kek.
School's free here.
You just bring your mind
and your smile
every day, OK?

Carefully I sit.
I like very much this new desk
with its cool, smooth top.

My mouth will not stop smiling.

READY

You're not going to understand
a lot of what we say at first, Ms. Hernandez says.
This is called an ESL class.
You and your classmates
will be learning English together.
It means they won't always
understand you.
And you won't always
understand them.

I'm used to not understanding, I say.
It's like playing a game
with no rules.

She nods.
That's exactly what it's like.
I know, because when I came
to the U.S. from Mexico,
I couldn't speak a word of English.

This is a surprise.
A teacher who did not know

all things?
Did you not know things also?
I ask Mr. Franklin.

Me? I'm from Baton Rouge, he says.
That's kinda like another country.
I couldn't understand
these crazy northern folks
for the longest time.

Some of his words get lost
on their way to my ears.
But I can see from his face
that his meaning is kind.

When you have a question,
Mr. Franklin and I will be
here to help, says Ms. Hernandez.
She points to the sky.
You just raise your hand
like this, OK?

I nod. I say, OK,
just like her.
I raise my hand.

Yes? she says, smiling big.

I ask,
When will the learning begin?

CATTLE

In my class,
my long-name class
called English-as-a-Second-Language,
we are sixteen.
Sixteen people
with twelve ways of talking.
When we talk at once
we sound like the music class
I can hear down the hall,
hoots and squeaks and thuds,
but no songs you can sing.

I look at our faces
and see all the colors of the earth—
brown and pink and yellow and white and black—
and yet we are all sitting at the same desks,
wanting to learn the same things.

Ms. Hernandez
tells everyone my name
and my old home.
Then she asks us

to draw a picture
on the black wall
to show where we come from.

One boy,
Jaime from Guatemala,
draws a mountain with a hole
called a volcano.
Sahar from Afghanistan
draws a camel,
though to be truthful
it looks like a lumpy dog.

I draw a bull with great curving horns,
like the finest in my father's herd.
I even give him a smile.
But it takes me a while
to decide on his coat.
In my words
we have ten different names
for the color of cattle.
But the writing chalk is only white.

I am working on the tail
when someone in the back of the room says,

Moo.
Then more say it,
and more,
and soon we are
a class of cattle.

At last we can all
understand each other.

I think maybe some of the students
are laughing at me.
But I don't mind so much.

To hear the cattle again
is good music.

LUNCH

After much schooling,
a sound comes
like a great bee buzzing.
The bell means lunch,
Mr. Franklin explains.
He gives me a small piece
of blue paper.
This is for your food.

Thank you very much,
I say in my most polite English words,
but I don't understand how the
paper can help my noisy belly.

You give the paper
to the cooking people
and they will give you food, Mr. Franklin explains.
Tastes much better than paper.
He laughs. Well, usually, anyway.

The eating room is grand
with long tables

and strange and wonderful smells
and many students chattering.
I stand in a line
and soon kind, white-hatted people
fill my plate high with food.

Ahead of me
I see the snowball girl named Hannah
from my building.
She says, Don't eat the mystery meat
if you value your life.
Then she points to a brown wet pile
on my plate and makes a face that says
bad taste.

When my tray is heavy
with the gifts of food,
I stand still in the
stream of students.
I don't know where to go
to enjoy my feast.

Hannah waves.
Follow me, she says.

I'll tell you what's
safe to eat.

But it's all so fine! I say.

She shakes her head.
Kid, you got a lot to learn.

FRIES

We sit at one of the long tables.
Nearby are two students
from my class:
Jaime, the boy from Guatemala
and Nishan, the girl from Ethiopia.
Hey, Jaime says.

Hey, I say back,
but I can't talk anymore
because my mouth is already
full of new tastes.

Excuse me, I say when I have swallowed at last,
but what is this amazing food?
I hold up a brown stick.

Fry, Hannah says.
One of the five major food groups.

This fry,
it grows in your
America ground? I ask.

Hannah laughs,
a sound like bells
on a windy day.
I suppose you could say that.
You're Kek, right?
I know because
I asked your cousin.

Hannah passes me a paper cup
filled with strange and beautiful red food.
Ketchup, she says.
You dip your fries in it.

I do what she says,
then eat.
You're a fine cook, I say.
Hannah and Jaime and Nishan laugh.
I feel glad I found enough words
to make people happy.
When a friend laughs,
it's always a good surprise.

NOT KNOWING

I see your cousin
at the apartments sometimes, Hannah says.
He's a very quiet guy.

I have to think for a moment.
To eat such happy food
and think about words
at the same time
is much work.

Ganwar, I say, has many worries.

He seems kind of sad, Hannah says.

I look at the fry in my hand
with its shiny coat of red.
I want only to eat,
and not to remember.
But Hannah's words
tug like tight rope
on a calf's neck.

Ganwar lost his father and his sisters
when the fighting came, I tell her.

Hannah nods. Her eyes
are blue and gray,
or maybe green. I can't be sure.
I remember a kind doctor at the camp
with such eyes.

How did he lose his hand? Hannah asks in a gentle voice.

I don't know the words
for this.
Some English words I hope
I never learn.

Men came with guns and knives
to our village, I answer at last.

To be in such fighting,
says Nishan,
is very bad.

And what about your family?
Jaime asks me.

I stop eating.
I take a breath.
My father and my brother, Lual,
they were killed
by the government men.
I saw it.

I pause,
as a memory pokes at me
like a knife in my back.
I was lucky to see, I add.

Lucky? Hannah asks.
Her voice says
she doesn't understand.

Nishan looks at me with
eyes that know of such things.
Maybe Kek means lucky
to know for sure, she explains.
Not knowing,
it's the hardest.

Yes, I agree.
The hardest.

How about your mom? Hannah asks softly.

I . . .
Guilt grabs my throat.
I will not go to that
black place today.

I try again.
She'll come, I say.
I'll wait here for her.

Waiting is hard, too,
Hannah says,
and I can see that she
also knows sad places.

I push my tray away.
I'm not so hungry anymore.

HOME

I take the school bus home.
It's a long yellow car
filled with screaming, laughing students
and many paper balls wet with spit.
I don't think it would be easy
to drive such a car.

My aunt is sleeping when I get home.
Ganwar enters with a white basket
under his arm.
The washing machine's in the basement, he says.

The what? I ask.

The room way down at the bottom of the stairs.
I'll show you later.
He surprises me with a smile like
Lual might have made,
a big-brother-making-trouble smile.
You'll like doing the wash.
It's my job, but if you want,
I might let you help.

Sure, I say,
although I don't
trust that mischief smile.
I remember well how Lual and Ganwar
used to tease and test me.
Always I was the little child
with foolish ideas and silly ways.
Always they were too old
to bother with me,
unless it was for their own fun.

The door to my aunt's room opens
and she comes out slowly,
yawning and stretching.
How was school? she asks.

You would not believe it, I say.
They teach you and feed you
and I have my own desk.
We're going to visit the zoo
where animals live
and the plan . . .
plan-et-arium . . .
where stars live.

And I'm going to learn how to
dunk-slam in the class called PE.

Slam-dunk, Ganwar corrects.

Good, my aunt says, good boy,
and she fills a kettle with water
to put on the cooking fire.
I want to tell her more,
but I can see
that her mind is visiting other places.

I think maybe I'll like
living here in America, I say to Ganwar.

Yeah, that's what I thought, too.
But you'll never really feel like an American,
Ganwar says. You'll see.

Why? I ask.

Ganwar shrugs.
Because they won't let you.

He tosses the basket on the sofa.

I'm outta here, he says, switching to English.

Be home by—
my aunt begins,
but Ganwar is already gone.

TIME

My aunt sighs and leans against the counter.
He's just not happy here, she says.
I know it's been hard for him.
But he doesn't try.
She rubs her eyes.
I have to go work, Kek. I've got an early shift.
Eat what you like and go to bed by eight.

I learned o'clocks at the camp, I say.
It is called time telling.
But why not use the sun and the stars?

My aunt points to the tiny clock
strapped to her arm.
Here in America, this is the sun.
You'll get used to it.
For now, just get some sleep.

I watch her put on her heavy coat.
She isn't even at work yet,
and already she's tired.

I go to the door with her.
Are you . . .
I stop, then try again.
Are you glad that you're here?

My aunt seems surprised that I would ask
such a question. She thinks for a moment.

The freedom is a great gift,
she says. To choose your leaders.
To walk the streets unafraid.
But it's lonely here.
And . . . she hesitates. Hard.
To change when you are older,
to learn new words and new ways,
that is big work.
But for you and Ganwar,
it will be easier.
That's my hope, anyway.

I watch through the window
as she tracks a path

through new snow falling.
Her footprints catch the flakes,
then vanish like
pebbles in quicksand.

HELPING

When my aunt leaves,
the apartment grows hushed
as the air before a storm.
I turn on the TV machine
but the words are too fast coming.

My aunt had looked so weary.
I wonder how I can help.
In the cooking fire room
are many dirty dishes.
Maybe I can clean them for my aunt.
I've seen her wash some plates in the sink
with bubbles.
But now there are many dishes
stacked high.

Ganwar said the machine for washing
was in the way-down-at-the-bottom-of-the-stairs-room.
Maybe that's what his
basket is for.

Carefully I place the
cups and saucers and plates
in the basket.
With my special key,
I lock the apartment door
just as Dave warned me to do.
Then I carry the basket of dishes
down the stairs
to the room of washing.

It's good to be a helping person.
If my father were here,
he would be proud, I think.
An ache in my chest comes,
throbbing like an old bruise.

The way-down room
smells like a rainy day.
I see six white boxes with doors.
Some are making noise.
I find a sleeping one and open the top.

One by one I put the dishes into the hole.
Then I close the top
and wait,
while all around me
the machines hum and talk.

HOW NOT TO WASH DISHES

Just then Hannah appears
in the doorway.
She's carrying a basket of clothes
and a big red bottle.
Hey, she says. What's up?

I look at the ceiling.

No, that means
what's new, what's going on?
She laughs. You must feel like I do
in Spanish class.

The machine isn't working, I say.

Did you put four quarters in? Hannah asks.
She reaches into her pocket
and pulls out shiny circles.
Money, she explains.
It makes the machine go.
She laughs her good laugh.

Actually, it makes the world go.
Here, I'll lend you a buck.

I can't accept such a gift, I begin,
but she just waves her hand.
You can pay me back later.

She places the four money pieces
into special holes in the machine,
then pushes them.
Noise begins,
like a tiny river flowing.
It's working! I cry.

Technology at its finest, she says.
Course you still have to dry it all,
then fold it.

Fold it? I ask. But I don't
understand—

I'll show you. Let me sort these clothes real quick.
Hey, you doing anything after this?
We could go upstairs and catch some TV
while we wait.

That would be good, I say.
I would like something to do.
Ganwar and my aunt aren't home.

My mom either. Well, she's not exactly my mom.
She's my foster mom.
She works the four to midnight
shift at the Quick Stop. She pauses.
That means she works at night,
kind of like your aunt.

I watch as Hannah pushes white clothes
into another machine.
These machines, they wash
clothes and dishes? I say,
shaking my head.
Mama will be amazed
when she sees this!

Hannah looks up.
Did you say—
but just then the river sound stops
and my machine begins to shake
like a crazed dancer under a full moon.

It's eating my dishes! I cry.
Please make it stop!

Hannah lifts the top of the machine.
The horrible noise
of its giant teeth stops.
She peers inside.

Whoa, she says.
I think this is what they call
a problem with translation.

NOT-SMART BOY

I don't want to cry.
A man must show strength
in the presence of a woman.
But if I had to choose
between kissing a crocodile
and telling my aunt
the news of her broken dishes,
I would choose the crocodile
any day.

I look into the hole.
Hannah looks, too.
It is not a good thing to see.
I have many more dishes.
But they are much smaller.

I look at Hannah.
She looks at me.
I cannot say why,
but when I look at her
I feel like I've gulped down
a laugh that needs to fly free.

I laugh, then she laughs,
then before I know it
we're on the hard floor
laughing.

Perhaps this is my punishment for
trying to do the work of a woman, I say,
wiping a tear away.

Hannah punches my shoulder.
Hey, in this country,
a woman can do anything a man can do.
She gets to her feet and grins.
This is your punishment for being a moron.

A moron is a not-smart boy? I ask.

She laughs. You got it.

I laugh, too.
I stand and pull out a piece of a plate.
Maybe I can fix these?

Well, I s'pose we can glue
some of the pieces together.

Put them in your basket
and we'll see what we can do.
But don't get your hopes up.

I'm used to hearing that, I say.

MAGIC MILK

I carry the broken pieces
in my basket and follow Hannah
to her apartment.
She has a key like mine
around her neck on a string.

Hannah's place of living is not like my aunt's.
It smells of many things,
some not so good.
Everywhere are clothes and shoes,
papers and dirty dishes.

Sorry. It's a dump, I know.
Hannah sighs.
My last foster parents
were total neat freaks.

Do you have brothers or sisters? I ask.

Three older. One boy, two girls. All foster.
My brother's working at Burger King right now.

Don't know what my sisters are up to.
My real brother lives with another family
in St. Paul.

Hannah begins opening drawers
in the cooking fire room.
I know we've got some glue somewhere, she says.

Forgive me, I say,
but I don't know what is a foster.

Foster family. You stay with them
when your real family is messed up.
My mom's in rehab and my dad's, well . . .
he hasn't been around since I was a baby.
She pauses. Sorry. I forget
it's hard to understand me sometimes.
Rehab is where you go if you do too much
alcohol or drugs.

I have seen men in our village
drink until they fall down
and laugh too loudly, I offer.

Hannah nods.
Yeah, like that.

Your mother will be well soon?

I doubt it, she says.
She looks at me.
Her eyes are wet, just a little.

You can't be sure
what will happen, I say.
Life changes. So you must hope.

I want so much to believe my words.

Hannah doesn't answer.
She opens the tall cold box.
Want some chocolate milk?

I know about chocolate.
At the camp, a helping doctor
gave me a small piece to try.
This is what laughing tastes like,
I told her.

I would like the milk very much, I say to Hannah.
I watch while she pours
wondrous brown milk
from a tall thin box.
In the camp, people told me
America was a great country, I say.
But I never dreamed you
would have cows that give such milk!

Hannah groans. The world's oldest joke, she says,
but I don't understand her meaning.

Where do you find this milk? I ask.

Grocery store. I'll take you sometime.
I take the bus there a lot.

The yellow school bus?

Nope. She shakes her head. City bus.

I sigh. I'll never know all the things
there are to know.

Hannah tilts her head to one side.
Don't worry. It'll get easier.
I'll help you.

How come you are so helping to me? I ask.

Hannah thinks for a minute. I dunno.
Guess I've moved around a lot myself.
Not like you. But I kind of know what it's like
to *not* know things.

She clinks her glass against mine.
Here's to Krazy Glue.

I don't understand those words, either.
But I don't care.
My mouth is too busy
rejoicing.

WET FEET

Even the wonder of Krazy Glue
can't turn my aunt's dishes
into their old selves.

The next morning I tell my aunt
of my great mistake.
She makes her lips into a line
and closes her eyes,
but she doesn't say a word.
I would like it better
if she could find her mad voice.
Back in Africa, she and my uncle
would argue so fiercely
that their hut trembled.
The cattle are stampeding again,
the villagers would joke.

But now I think maybe she is too tired to yell.

When Dave comes to visit in the afternoon,
I tell him about the broken dishes.
He just laughs. That's nothing, he says.

I once had a client who tried to
wash his clothes in the toilet.

This doesn't sound like
such a wrong idea to me,
but I decide to hide my thinking.
Instead I say,
I must get a job, Dave, like my aunt.
So that I can buy her new dishes.

Hold on, he says.
We'll see about that soon enough.
You just got here, Kek.
You need some time to get your feet wet.

I check my shoes.
It's true enough that they are dry.

That's called an idiom, Dave explains.
You're going to run into a lot of those.
It means get some experience.

Dave turns to Ganwar,
who's sprawled on the couch
like a dozing dog.

Actually, I've been meaning to talk to *you*
about a job, buddy.
There are some openings
at a couple fast-food places
on the bus line.

Ganwar groans.
He doesn't bother
to open his eyes.
I didn't come to this country
to sweep the floors, he mutters.

You gotta start somewhere, Dave says.
And your mom needs some
help with the bills.
You're the man
of the family now.

A man doesn't wear a paper hat
and give out ketchup packets, Ganwar replies.

Ketchup is a fine food, isn't it? I offer,
but Ganwar ignores me.

Don't be intimidated, Ganwar, Dave says.
They'll teach you the skills you need.

I have many skills, Ganwar says.
Even with one hand.
His words spark like lightning.

Ganwar is a great herdsman, I say.
He was one of the
best in our village.

We'll talk about this later, Ganwar, Dave says.

I follow Dave to the door.
I want to ask him something.
But I am afraid he will say no.
I take a big breath.

Do you remember the cow
we saw that day? I ask.
I would like to go back and visit her again.

Gee, I can't today, Kek, Dave says. But maybe next week.

He did not say no, I realize.
So I try again,
just like I would have
with my own father.

Sometimes if you ask enough,
fathers turn maybe
into yes.

But only sometimes.

Maybe I could take the bus?
My new friend Hannah takes the bus
to many places, I say.
She could come with me.

Dave thinks for a moment.
He takes a little piece of paper and a pen
out of his coat pocket
and writes some words.
This is where the farm is.
But don't try going without
a friend to help you, OK?

OK, I say,
and I put the paper in the pocket of my jeans.

Give her a pat for me, buddy,
Dave says as he opens the door.
I think he is just being kind,
since I'm certain he is not a great lover of cows.

I wave good-bye and smile to myself
with the secret comfort
of a big idea.

BUS

On the day with the name of Saturday,
Hannah and I wait by the road
for the bus to come.
It's even bigger than the school bus,
with the sour breath and slow growl
of a starving animal.

The door squeals open and
I follow Hannah up the stairs.
She pours quarters into my glove.
Here, she says. Do like I do.
Her money clatters into a box by the driver.

But—
I shake my head.
The school bus is free.

This one you pay for, she says.
C'mon, hurry up.

The driver makes a face that says
stupid-new-to-this-country-boy.

But Hannah, I say,
I can't take more money from you.

Hannah tips my glove over the box
and the quarters slip in with a
happy jangle.
She grabs my arm as the bus
rushes forward.
We pile into a seat near the back.

See, my mom sends me money sometimes, Hannah says.
Her nose and cheeks are red as sunset sky.
Just, you know, out of the blue.
No explanation, no letter.
It just shows up.
I used to write her and say thanks,
but now I don't bother.
She never writes back.
Anyway, my foster mom always
hands the money over to me.
I give her some and then the rest
I put in a box under my bed.

But it's yours to spend, I say.
Not mine.

Hey, you get a job,
you can pay me back.
Meantime, keep your eyes open.

I blink. But they are—

I mean, look out the window for this farm.
I'm not sure if Dave's got
the right stop or not.
I never noticed a farm out this way.

It's a very small farm, I admit.

After much snow and many buildings,
I see at last the little farm.
The bus pulls over and
we step into a pile of snow
as high as our knees.

There she is, I say.
The cow is standing near a shed.
She looks bored. And cold.

I thought she was a girl, Hannah says.
She has horns.

Girl cattle can have horns, I explain.

Really? Hannah asks.
Way to go, girl cow.
So now what?

When I take a deep breath of icy air,
it is like swallowing an arrow.

Now, I say, I get my job.

LOU

It's a hard walk to the house
where the owner of the cow lives.
Much snow makes a home in my boots.
When we get to the door,
Hannah shows me a button
that makes music happen,
and soon the door opens.

The old woman standing there
doesn't seem surprised to see us.
Well, hello, she says. May I help you kids?

I am Kek, I say, from Africa.
And this is Hannah.

From Minneapolis, Hannah adds.

I'm Louise, the woman says.
From the wrong side of the tracks.
Call me Lou.
Weren't you here the other day,
talking to my cow?

I nod. I just wanted to say hello to her.

Lou thinks about this for a moment.
It's bitter out there. C'mon in.

We step into safe, warm air
and sweet cooking smells.
So, are you two selling something? Lou asks.
Raising money for school?

I'm here about your cow, I say.

I see. Lou nods slowly.

I think that she is
not so happy, I say.
I try to say it gently so that
my words will not sting like an insect.

Lou puts her hands on her hips.
She's wearing jeans like mine and a big shirt.
Her hair is short and silver
like a fresh moon.
She has many wrinkles

to show her great knowledge
of the world.

You two better sit. This may take some time.
Lou points to the kitchen table.
I was unaware that my cow's depressed.
Although I'm not entirely surprised.
She's seen better days.

Lou pushes a plate of cookies
in front of us.
Chocolate pieces tease
like jewels in sand.
Please, she says, have some.

I don't want to be impolite,
so I take five.

He's big on chocolate, Hannah explains.

Lou laughs. Now tell me, Kek,
how you come by your
knowledge of cows.

COWS AND COOKIES

Of course I want to answer,
but I know it's important to
eat all the cookies first,
so that Lou won't be offended.

Hannah helps. See, Kek just got here from Africa.
He's staying with his aunt and cousin,
and he accidentally put her dishes
in the washing machine
and now he needs some money
to buy new ones.
And since in Africa his family had lots of cattle,
he thought maybe you could use some help.
She pauses to take a bite of cookie,
and now she can't talk, either.

Hmmm, Lou says.
She goes to the cold tall box to get some milk.
I'm a little sad to see that the milk
is not the chocolate cow kind.
She pours the milk into glasses
and watches while we drink.

My husband's family came here from Norway, Lou says.
And my great-great grandfather came to the U.S.
on a boat from Ireland.
She pours herself a glass of milk.
But Africa. Wow. How are you handling winter?

The cold . . . hurts, I answer.
But the snowballs are good.

Lou smiles. So tell me why you think
my cow is unhappy.

It isn't because you don't care well for her, I say quickly.

Not as well as I should, Lou says.
My husband died last year, and with my
achy old bones, I'm having a hard time keeping up.
She picks up a cookie, but doesn't eat it.
I may have to sell the place soon. I had an offer,
a good offer. And I have a lot
of hospital bills to pay off.
I don't know. We'll see.

We're all quiet for a moment.

So, Lou says at last, what is it
you think my old cow is in need of?

She needs to be brushed, and fed the finest hay.
And without other cattle, she's lonely, I answer.
She needs someone to talk to her.
In my old home they would laugh at me,
but when I talked to the cattle,
they would grow calm and easy to herd.

I wait. Maybe my words are
broken like my aunt's dishes,
chips and shards
that will not make a whole.
Maybe this Lou will think
I am a moron boy.

Have another cookie, Kek, says Lou.

NIGHT TALK

That night I wait far into the darkness
for Ganwar to come home.
He stumbles a little when he crosses the room,
and he carries the bitter smell of smoke.
Where were you? I ask.

With some friends, he says,
and he plops onto the sofa
like a sack of grain.

I've been waiting for you, I say.
I wanted to tell you my news.
I got a job!

Ganwar lifts his head
to stare at me. A job?
Doing what?

Helping a lady take care of her farm.
For a while, at least.
She's old and her husband died last year.
She can't pay me very much,

but I think I'll
make enough to buy new dishes
for your mother.

Ganwar's eyes say I am telling a lie,
or maybe a joke.
How did you get a job like that?

I lift my shoulders. I just went to her door and asked.
Her cow didn't look good. Father would never
have owned such a sad-looking animal.

Ganwar drops his head
and covers his eyes with his hand.
Amazing. You just went to her door?

I nod.

I've been here a year and a half.
Ganwar sighs. You've been here—what?
A week?

We're quiet for a while.
I can hear the cold box humming.
I do not want Ganwar to be angry with me.

I want him to understand,
because he is the only one who can.

I miss the cattle, I say at last.
I miss moving them,
watching them graze.
The sun so hot on your back.
Father singing.

Ganwar doesn't answer.
I think maybe I should not talk of days past
with my cousin.
I cringe, waiting for the heat of his words.

Ganwar rubs his eyes.
When he speaks,
his voice is sad, not angry.
I always knew what to do, he says.
Morning they'd graze,
noon we'd lead them to a stream,
afternoon we'd head for home.
We always had somewhere to go.
Not like here, stuck in the apartment
or at school.

He sighs. It all made sense.
Here, nothing makes sense.

Maybe it will, I say.
Maybe if we're patient.
I hear the fear and hope fighting in my voice.

We don't belong here, Kek, Ganwar says.
This isn't our country.
It never will be.

Lots of people come to America from other countries,
I say. Ms. Hernandez taught us that.

Ganwar rolls his eyes.
Poor immigrants. Illegal immigrants.

Maybe someday we can go home again, I say.

The war is older than our fathers were.
The war is forever, Ganwar replies.
He closes his eyes.

Then where do we belong? I ask.
I can see that he's sleepy,
but I want Ganwar to tell me this one thing.

I wait a long time
for Ganwar to reply,
but he's asleep, snoring softly.

I watch his untroubled face.
I cannot seem to get up.
Ganwar's words lie in my lap
like huge rocks
I am not strong enough to move.

I sit and sit,
waiting for the sleep
my cousin has found,
wishing for dreams of our old life,
of fine, strong cattle
gently complaining
like tired children
as we guide them safely home.

PART THREE

*One doesn't forego sleeping
because of the possibility of nightmares.*

—AFRICAN PROVERB

COWBOY

In ESL class
we learn a new game
called Interview.
Ms. Hernandez says it makes us
more confident
when we use our English words.
Plus it's a good way to learn
about our classmates.

First we have to hold a cardboard tube
and pretend that it's
something called a microphone
to make our voices loud.
I saw one once on the TV machine
with a lady singing into it.
She howled like a sick animal
till my ears wanted to run away.

I'm the first to go.
I have to stand up and say five sentences.
I say, I have a new job.
I help Lou with her farm.
She has a cow, three goats, many chickens and a pig.
I will go there after school sometimes and on the days
named Saturday and Sunday.
Lou says I can name the cow.

I take a deep breath. I'm weary from my long speech.

Next comes the Interview part.
That is where each student asks you a question.
If they run out of questions,
then the teachers can help.

Nishan is first.
Why does the cow not have a name?

I take another deep breath.
I like the questions best
with yes or no for an answer,
but this time I'm not so lucky.

Lou says her husband called the cow
The Cow.
She didn't think that was
such a right name.

Very good answer, Kek,
says Mr. Franklin.

Aisha is next.
You could call the cow "Mr. Franklin."
The class thinks this is a good joke,
and there is much laughing.

She's a girl,
so she needs a girl name, I explain.

Now each person has an idea
for a name. This isn't exactly how to play
Interview, but the teachers
don't seem to mind.

Ms. Hernandez writes the names on the board.
Some are very silly:

Mr. Franklin
Milkshake
Ms. Hernandez
Kek, Jr.
Kitty Kitty
Salama
Rover
Chiku
Angelita
Zlata
Big Mac

When they're done, Mr. Franklin asks me
if I have a name in mind.

I think for a moment.
We have a word in my language, I say.
Gol.

And what does it mean? Mr. Franklin asks.

I feel my face heat.
It means *family,* I say.

Ms. Hernandez says it's up to me.
But I say I would like to have a vote,
because Ms. Hernandez taught us
that's how things are decided
in America.
We vote.
Gol wins.
Hamburger gets two votes.

Nice job, Cowboy, Mr. Franklin says
when I sit down
at last.

The rest of the day,
everyone calls me "Cowboy."

It's a good day.
The cow has a new name.
And I have one, too.

WORKING

The snow and muck yank at my boots.
The wind slaps my cheeks.
In my heavy coat I plod like an old donkey
on market day.

So why am I so glad in my heart?

The work at Lou's is simple:
feed the animals, clean the stalls,
shovel the front porch.
But when I am working, my mind doesn't travel
where it shouldn't go.
I'm only here,
with the chickens underfoot
and Gol nudging for an ear scratch.

Sometimes I talk to her softly.
I tell her of my father's great herd
and how they would graze each day,
walking for miles,
the sun in our bones,
the grass whispering its shy music.

I sing her one of my father's songs
and listen for an echo of his voice in mine.
She nuzzles me and flicks her ears
and chews her cud.

When I bury my face in Gol's old hide
I smell hay and dung and life.
She shelters me like a warm wall,
and that is enough for this day.

GANWAR, MEET GOL

On Saturday Dave comes to pick up Ganwar.
They're going to fill out paperwork
asking for a job
at the places that sell fries.
Dave says he can drop me off
at Lou's on the way.

Ganwar doesn't talk on the way to the farm.
His face looks frozen,
but his eyes are hot.
He keeps rubbing the place
where his hand once was.

When we get to Lou's, I say,
Would it be all right if I showed Ganwar the farm?
He hasn't seen a cow in a long time.

I wait for Ganwar
to spit out the word *no,*
but he gives a slow nod.
Dave looks at his arm clock.
Ten minutes, he says, tops.

We go to Lou's door and when she opens it I say,
This is my cousin, Ganwar.
He'd like to see the farm.

Be my guest, Lou says.
There's a new bag of chicken feed
in the shed, Kek.

Ganwar follows me
through the thick, crunching snow.
It isn't much of a farm, he says.
Hardly any animals, and the big road so near.

Still, it isn't so bad
if you don't think about it,
I say. I shake my head.
I'm getting very good at
not thinking about things.

We enter the gray, sagging barn.
Sun and angry wind sneak through the broken spots.
There she is, I say, pointing.

Ganwar groans.
Are you sure that's a cow?

Our fathers wouldn't think so, I admit.
I stroke her flank while Ganwar watches.
She has old eyes, tired but patient.
Gol is her new name, I add.

Ganwar takes his glove off his good hand
with his teeth.
He strokes her, too.
I meet Ganwar's eyes.
Don't worry about the job too much, I say.
What another man takes two hands to do,
you can do with one.

Ganwar puts his head
against Gol's neck.
You're lucky to have found this job.
But you made the luck happen.

I wish I could be herding, I say.
I don't know anything about farms, really.
Except that they have cows.

We stand there,
watching the cow's breath
come in soft puffs.

Suddenly another big idea
jumps into my head.

I think that if I knew where such ideas come from,
I would be a wealthy man
with a thousand cattle
and a flying boat.

Stay here, I say.
Keep her company for me.

AN IDEA

A few minutes later I race back to the barn,
stumbling in the stubborn snow.

Dave and Lou follow.
Lou has on a thick red coat
and a hat with a fuzzy ball on top.

Ganwar is still leaning against Gol.
You cousin has an idea, says Dave.

My grin is so big it hurts.
You can work with me here! I exclaim.
Helping with the farm!

All is quiet.
Ganwar looks doubtful.
He doesn't say yes,
but he doesn't say no, either.

I don't have much cash, Lou says.
You'd have to split
the pay I'd promised Kek.

But come spring I sell
organic veggies and flowers
at the farmers' market,
and you could help with that.
She pauses. Assuming, that is,
I hang onto this old place.

Ganwar looks at me hard.
I can't take your charity.

But I'm taking yours, I say.
You're sharing your home with me.

I don't know anything about farming, Ganwar says.

I don't either, I say.

Ganwar turns to Lou and holds out his hurt arm.
What about this? he asks.
His voice is soft,
but his words are shouting.

We all look at Lou.
Lou shrugs.
Guess you'll have to use the other one, she says.

For some reason
this makes Ganwar smile.
He slowly nods.
He glances at Dave.
Can you come back later? he asks.
We have dung to shovel.

I laugh.
It's much harder here, I warn him.
Everything freezes.
Even that.

Gol moos softly,
as if she's sorry to make work for us.

Dave shakes my hand, then Lou's, then Ganwar's.
Folks, this is great, he says.
Ganwar, don't let Lou down, buddy.

He won't, Lou says.
She winks.

Dave and Lou leave us
in the cold barn.
I look around me.

It's not a great herd I see,
dotting the grass
like clouds in a vast green sky.
It's just a tired flock
of scrawny chickens
and a cow with ribs trying to hide
behind her muddy coat.

But for a moment,
as Ganwar and I hum
one of the old songs,
we are where we belong
in the world.

FIELD TRIP

The next week,
my ESL class takes a field trip to the zoo.
Field trip is another English trick,
like *raining cats and dogs*
and *a barrel of laughs*
because there is no field
and it's not a far trip
like the one I took from Africa.

We take a yellow bus.
When we get to the zoo,
we must stand in line to get our tickets.
The other kids complain,
but I am used to lines.
One day in the refugee camp
I stood in line for nine hours
to get a handful of corn.

At last a guiding lady walks us past
birds and lizards,
fish and butterflies,

zebras and elephants.
We're looking for animals
from our homelands.

I see gazelles
standing on a low hill
beyond a fence.
I remember such animals bounding
through tall grass,
riding the air like
wingless birds.
I wonder,
How did they come to be here in this strange, cold world?
They flick their tails
and check the horizon for danger.
They're safe here,
but they don't know it.

We visit the petting zoo,
with its animals for touching
who will not eat your hand.
There are goats and chickens and pigs,
a llama and a turkey,
but no cows.

We are supposed to be watching the animals,
but I can't stop looking at the people
looking at all the animals.

A class of little children
laughs at the pigs
rolling happily in cold mud.
Their class looks like our class,
or maybe we look like them:
many colors and shapes
and words.

Of all the things I didn't know
about America,
this is the most amazing:
I didn't know
there would be so many tribes
from all over the world.
How could I have imagined
the way they walk through the world
side by side
without fear,
all free to gaze at the same sky
with the same hopes?

What would my father have said,
to see such a thing? My brother?

What will my mother say?

I walk behind my classmates to the next exhibit,
but I am not alone.
My family is with me,
and every sight is something they cannot see,
and every hope is something they cannot feel.

To carry them, unseen as wind,
is a heavy burden.

THE QUESTION

All afternoon my belly aches.
Maybe I should have eaten more, I tell myself.
But I know the hurt of hunger well.
Hunger is a wild dog
gnawing on a dry bone,
mad with impatience
but hoping still.

It isn't hunger I feel today.
This pain is worse,
one without pity
like an icy night.
This pain is a question,
the one my heart will not stop asking:
Why am I here,
when so many others are not?
Why should I have a desk
and a pair of fine jeans
and a soft place for my head to rest?
Why should I have the freedom to hope
while my brother and father
sleep in bloodied earth?

I should not take these gifts
I do not deserve.
And yet I know I will take them,
warm food
and soft bed
and fresh hope,
holding on tight
as that wild dog
to his bone.

APPLE

Before ESL we have homeroom.
I don't much like it.
In my homeroom are only
three other ESL students,
and I don't speak their words.
All the rest are from America.

One morning,
a folded paper waits on my homeroom desk.
I think maybe it's a note to pass.
I've seen other students
hand paper to each other
during the loud man in the wall
named Announcements.
It's exciting to think
I might already have a homeroom friend.

When I open it, I see a picture.
It's not a good drawing.
But after a moment I can see
it's a dead body made of bones.

Hungry, Kenya? a boy in the back asks.
His voice has knives in it.
He holds up an apple half eaten.

None for me, thank-you, I say,
using my polite English words.
And my home, I add,
is not Kenya. It's Sudan.

He tosses the apple across the room.
It lands on my desk
and drops to the floor.

My homeroom teacher
looks up from his newspaper.
Can the flying fruit, he says.

Of course, I don't want
the apple to be wasted.
I pick it up off the floor
and throw it back to the boy.

It hits him on the nose.

I'm a fine thrower of rocks and balls.
It is not my fault the boy moved.

The teacher gives me a detention slip.
I'm not sure what this slip means,
but I do know I'm the only one in class
who receives one.

I feel very lucky
to be selected by my teacher
for such an honor.

GROCERY STORE

The next afternoon,
Hannah invites me
to visit the grocery store with her.
Her mother she calls a foster has asked her
to buy some food for dinner.

We take another bus to a place
of many cars in neat rows.
By the time we get there
the sun has already said good night.
That's it, Hannah says.
Safeway.

There isn't enough food in the world
to fill such a building, I say.

I follow her inside,
and she grabs a shiny cart.
You don't pay for this fine cart? I ask.

You just borrow it, she explains.

The grocery store
has rows and rows
of color, of light,
of easy hope.
Hannah moves down the aisle,
but I stand like a tree rooted firm,
my eyes too full of this place,
with its answers to prayers
on every shelf.

Hannah glances over her shoulder.
You OK? she asks.
I reach out and touch
a piece of bright green food
I've never seen before.
And then I begin to cry.

Hannah rushes to my side.
It's OK, she says.
We can leave if you want.

She takes my hand
and we leave the empty cart
and go outside.
We sit on the icy bench

and wait for the bus.
A car whooshes past.
Its lights cut the gloom
like the eyes of a great cat
prowling for food
in the moonlight.

THE STORY I TELL HANNAH ON THE WAY HOME

In our tent in the camp
a baby was dying.
Flies teased her eyes
and her arms hung
like broken sticks.
Her mother was
not much older than I am.
All day long she
whispered to the baby
drink, drink, drink.
All day, all night.
We couldn't sleep
for the sound of it.

But the baby had been hungry
for too long
and the bottle
went untouched
and after a while
the mother stopped rocking
and went silent.

When the baby died,
she covered her child
with a feed sack
and she said to no one,
I told her to eat.
Why wouldn't she eat?

When I'm done with the story,
I stare out the window
at the sunless world.

Hannah stares with me.
This time, she's the one
who cannot find any words.

LIBRARY

Ms. Hernandez and Mr. Franklin
take us to the school library twice a week.
It's filled with books on shelves,
climbing to the ceiling like
little buildings.
Each book is like a door
waiting to be unlocked.

Today I sit at a table
but I don't pick a book to read
like everyone else in my class.
Today,
I don't know why,
feels like the day at the grocery store.

Today I'm thinking of how my mother
always wanted to learn to read,
to own a book,
to open one of these magical presents
and see what's inside.

Ms. Hernandez shows me a book about cows.
She asks me to find a picture of a cow like Gol,
but I tell her I don't feel
in a library mood
today.

That's OK, she says. I know how that goes.

It's just so hard to choose, I add.
There are so many books.
And where I come from,
there are hardly any.

Ms. Hernandez nods.
I felt that way a lot
when I first came here.
Once I went to the mall and ended up
hiding in the corner of a clothes store.
It was just too many lights,
too many clothes, you know?
And I still feel kind of funny at movies.
Have you been to a movie yet?

I shake my head. Not one of the big movies.
But I did see a little one

on the flying boat.
I went to a grocery store, though.
I started to—
I whisper the last word—
cry.

Ms. Hernandez pats my hand.
It's just too much sometimes, isn't it?
When you had almost nothing.
And when you know that many people
still have so little.

I don't know what to do with it all, I say.
I kick at a chair leg.
To have all this food and
all these books
and all this freedom.
I feel sort of . . .
I don't know the word.
Too lucky.

It's a big gift, she agrees.

I reach for the cow book.
My father would have liked
this book, I say.

I'd like to hear
about your family, Ms. Hernandez says.

I think for a minute.
My father was a fine singer, I say.

Tell me more, Ms. Hernandez says.
And I do.

GOING UP

Time passes,
the kind they call *weeks*.
I have a little money from my job.
I have to make myself believe that a
crumpled piece of green paper
means something,
means anything.
In my old world, it was easy—
you could know a person's
wealth by counting his cattle.

Hannah and I take the bus
to a giant store filled with many things to buy.
I've promised her
I will not get upset this time.
I want to buy my aunt some new dishes.

There are stores within stores here
and music and food.
It's bright and big,
with toys and chairs,

TV machines and T-shirts.
What do you call such a place? I ask.

The mall, Hannah replies.

I follow her to a huge shiny store.
I've herded cattle for hundreds of miles
with only the stars to guide me.
But I'm certain I could never
find my way out of this place.

Hannah takes me to two magic silver staircases,
one going up,
one coming down.
I watch as the stairs melt away,
then reappear.
It's just an escalator, she says.
No big deal. C'mon.

I shake my head. They had these at the airport,
but Dave let me take the stairs instead.
Is there another way to climb?

She laughs. Well, there's an elevator.

That would be a better way, I think.

OK, but you gotta promise me you'll try it
next time. It's fun, Hannah says.
So are elevators.

The elevator is hiding near a row
of puffy white coats,
like clouds with arms.
Hannah pushes a button.
We wait.
A bell rings, and then
the doors vanish.
I follow her into the little room
waiting for us.
She pushes another button,
then—*zoom!*—
up we fly.

I think I left my stomach
downstairs, I say.

Hannah smiles.
Told you it was fun.

HEARTS

Hannah leads me to shelves
full of colorful dishes.
I like some with many stripes,
but she says I can't afford them.
She picks out a small box of white ones.
This should pretty much
replace what you broke, Hannah says.

I cradle the box gently in my arms.
the way I would carry a newborn calf.
On the way to the paying place,
we pass many red sparkling cards
and much candy.
Some of it is even chocolate.
Valentine's Day is in a couple days,
Hannah explains.
You give stuff to people you like.
Plus it just happens to be
my birthday.
Hey, when's your birthday?

I don't know, I admit. We don't
have birthdays in the way that you do.
But I know I was born in the time
you call summer.
Hannah looks confused by this news.
It's hard for me to remember
that she sometimes finds my ways
as strange as I find hers.

I must find you a gift, I say.
After I pay you back the money I owe
for the bus and the washing,
how much do I have left?

No way, Hannah says.
You're not spending your
hard-earned money on yours truly.

But it would make me very proud, I argue.
And it's my duty as your friend.

Hannah grins out of one side of her mouth,
a silly tilted smile
like a new moon rising.

OK, OK. See that little box of heart candy?
You could afford that.

It must be chocolate,
I say firmly.

She scans the shelves.
Here, she says at last.
She hands me a shiny little heart.
Perfect.

We stand in a long line.
When I give the lady my money
for the dishes and the heart,
my own heart grows so big with pride
I fear it might pop open
like a ripe seedpod.

I earned this money, I tell her.
I take care of a cow.
It's a fine job.

The lady smiles politely.
If you say so, hon.

Again I'm learning
that America people
don't understand the wonder of a cow.
Maybe if they had more cows
on the TV machine,
people would begin to feel
as Ganwar and I do.

You can have your dogs and cats,
your gerbils and hamsters
and sleek sparkling fish.
But you will have lived
just half a life
if you never love a cow.

WHITE GIRL

In front of our apartment,
I give the shiny heart to Hannah.
Happy birthday and Happy Valentine's Day, I say,
to my good friend, Hannah.

Three boys walk past
just as Hannah slips the silver heart
into the pocket of her coat.
They glare at us with eyes that shoot poison.
Leave the white girl alone, one yells.
Hands off, boy.

Just ignore them, Hannah whispers.
She pulls me inside
and slams the door shut.
A moment later,
she opens it a crack
and peers out.

They're gone, she says.

I shake my head. I don't understand, I say.

Me neither, Hannah says.
Me, neither.

You shouldn't have pulled me inside, I mutter.

They're jerks. Hannah yanks off her mittens.
I didn't want you to get hurt.

I am a man, I say, standing tall.

Sure you are, Hannah says.
I just . . . you know,
didn't see the point
in a fight.
Why does it matter?

I can't explain.
Suddenly I feel tired of using words
that don't belong to me.
Never mind, I say.
I trudge up the stairs.

My aunt is surprised to see
the box from me.
A present, she keeps saying,
a present for me?
She opens the dishes
and hugs me hard.
You are such a fine boy, Kek, she says.

I feel happy about the dishes
and bad about the angry boys.
It's hard to feel two things at once
so I try not to feel anything.

I sit next to Ganwar on the sofa.
Together we watch the TV machine
tell its happy, easy stories.

SCARS

Every weekend and other days sometimes
Ganwar and I go to Lou's.
It feels good to go
somewhere simple,
to work and sing
and eat cookies with chocolate.

Ganwar doesn't say so,
but I think he is calmer
on these days.
Sometimes he even
whistles a radio song,
or tells me jokes in English
that I don't understand.
Always, though, I laugh
to make him happy.

One afternoon Ganwar and I
rebuild a gate that's rotted away
at the edge of the field.
It's long work
and we sweat under our thick coats.

The sun is still weary and weak,
like a traveler too long on the road.
But each day it's trying harder
to warm the world.

Ganwar wipes away sweat with his arm.
The six lines
etched in his forehead
glisten.

I will never have the *gaar*, I say suddenly.
My words surprise me.
It's an idea I've never let myself
think about until now.
The initiation ceremony is
part of another place—
a place I may never return to.

You're lucky, Ganwar says.
Why would you want such scars?
Here they mean nothing.

There they meant everything, I say.
I lean on the fence.
How will I know when I'm a man?

Ganwar keeps hammering.
When you own a fine car
and a house with many bathrooms,
then you're a man in this country,
he answers with a smile.

It isn't so funny, I say.
You've been tested, and I haven't.
You were brave.
I look away. I don't want him to see
my eyes and what lies hidden there.
Me, I haven't been.

Sure you have, Ganwar replies.
You were in the camp alone,
you came here alone.
That's plenty brave.
It doesn't take a knife in the hand
of a village elder for you to prove
yourself.

I pick up my hammer
and slam it hard against a
rusty nail sticking out of the wood.
That's easy for you to say.

After that, I won't talk anymore.
But I hammer many nails
as hard as I can.
Even with my gloves on,
I have a good, hurting blister
to show for it.

BAD NEWS

More weeks pass. Something strange
is happening to the world.
I hear birdsong now, where only
silence filled the air before.
Tiny green hints
dot the trees and bushes.
The snow is getting smaller and grayer,
like an old person whose time is past.

Dave says it's called spring.

One morning, Lou calls
us to come into her kitchen.
A plate of warm chocolate cookies
waits for us.
I'm happy about this,
until I see Lou's ankle,
covered by a thick white bandage.

Sprained the dang thing last night, she says.
Slipped in the barn.

Do you have many pains? I ask.

Nah. She waves away the question
like a troublesome insect.
But it's gotten me to thinking, boys.
Even with your help, I just can't keep
this place running anymore.
Wish it weren't that way.
I've been here a long, long time.
It's time to sell and move on.

Ganwar nods. He doesn't look surprised.
It's OK, Lou.
We knew it probably wouldn't last.

I stare out the window.
Where will you go, I ask in a whisper,
when the farm is sold?

Lou lifts her shoulders. I'm not sure.
This has been my home so long,
I don't know anywhere else.
I have a sister in Los Angeles.
She makes a face.

Not sure I could stand all that nice weather.
What would I complain about?

We can stay on
as long as you need us, Ganwar says.
He doesn't sound mad at all.
He sounds like he is used to being disappointed.

But what about Gol? I ask.
My voice has a crack in it.

Lou looks out the window, too.
I don't know, Kek.
They're going to build a strip mall.
Won't be needing a cow, I'm guessing.
She sighs.
Gol is a very old, tired animal.
I don't think we'll probably be able
to find anyone who wants her.
I'm sorry, hon.

I leap to my feet.
My chair falls back with a loud thud.
I hate it here! I scream.
I want to go home!

I run out the door and across the field
toward the bus stop.
I'm glad that Lou can't follow me
with her sore foot.
I'm sorry that I'm glad.
And I'm mad that Ganwar isn't mad enough.

NO MORE

I stop working at Lou's.
Ganwar keeps going to the farm.
But he doesn't say anything to me about it.

When he comes home with hay and mud
stuck to the bottom of his running shoes,
I leave the room.

Lou calls for me on my aunt's telephone
to see if I will change my mind,
but I won't talk to her.
She tells my aunt I'm a hard worker.
She says she and Gol miss my smile.

One morning Mr. Franklin says,
Hey, Cowboy,
and I almost start to cry.

I say, Please don't call me that
anymore.
I am just Kek now.
But I don't tell him why.

Hannah says I am
cutting off my nose to spite my face.
I don't know what this means,
so she explains:
It means you are being a stubborn
moron boy.

She looks a little sad when she says this,
so I don't get mad at her.
Why don't you at least keep going
for a while? she asks.
It could be months before she leaves.

Because at the end I know
Lou and Gol and the farm
will be gone forever, I say.
Can't you understand this feeling?

Hannah chews on her lip.
Yeah, I guess I can, she says at last.

I wonder if maybe she is
thinking about her mother
who is not a foster.
But I don't ask.

LAST DAY

The days warm and the world
begins again.
I think of Gol nosing the ground,
grateful to find tender grass
appearing at her feet.

After spring, Ganwar says,
comes the time called summer
and no school
and sun strong
as a young man.

He says Lou may not leave until summer ends.
But I close my ears to his words.

The last day of school
Ms. Hernandez and Mr. Franklin
put our desks into a circle.
Ms. Hernandez stands in the middle.
Here comes a speech, she says.
We all groan.

That noise is the same in all languages.
She laughs.
I promise it'll be a very short speech.
I just want you to know
that I'm very proud of all of you.
You have learned much and
come far this year.

She makes a funny sound in her throat,
but I do not think she has a cold.

Like so many immigrants before you,
I know you'll help make this country
a better, stronger place.
She wipes her eyes. OK.
Speech over.

Mr. Franklin brings over a big box
and places it on a desk.
Inside is a cake,
an amazing long cake.
I wonder if maybe it's the
biggest cake in the world.
Ta-da! he says.

In the middle of the cake
is a green lady with her arm
in the air.
She's holding
a green candle.

Anybody recognize this ol' gal?
Mr. Franklin asks.

The Statue of Liberty!
everyone yells at once.

Why is she falling over?
Jaime asks.

Hey, I'm a teacher, not a baker,
says Mr. Franklin.

Maybe she's tired,
Ms. Hernandez suggests.
She has a big job, after all.

Why does she have a dog? Pedro asks.

Mr. Franklin sighs loudly.
That isn't a dog.
It's a cow.
It's supposed to be Gol.
He shrugs. I thought it would
be a nice touch.

I look away.
I still haven't told anyone at school
that Gol will soon be gone.

There are words all over the cake
in green letters. Many words in squiggles.
Before we eat,
Ms. Hernandez says,
we read.

Everyone groans again,
but she holds a finger to her lips
and you know that means business.

Mr. Franklin lights the candle,
and Ms. Hernandez
makes her voice extra soft

so that we will pay attention.
That is a trick teachers like to use.

These are important words, she says.
They mean that
this is your country,
now and forever:

Give me your tired, your poor,
Your huddled masses yearning to breathe free,
The wretched refuse of your teeming shore.
Send these, the homeless, tempest-tost to me.
I lift my lamp beside the golden door.

The candle glows
in the green lady's hand,
and I don't understand all the words,
but somehow I know
they're strong and fine.
I wonder if someday it will feel
like they are meant for me, too.

And then we eat the cake.
All of it.
Except Gol.

SUMMER

I would not be truthful
if I said that winter
is my favorite time.
Winter is wet and heavy work.
True, I learned to make snowballs
like perfect moons
and to catch a snowflake
on my tongue.
But I grew weary of looking
for missing gloves.

After such a winter,
summer comes like a present with a bow.
Summer is ice cream and skateboards
and sweet grass under your
free toes.
And just as Dave promised,
the not-dead trees had been teasing me.
Their leaves stop hiding
and over my head they weave
a cool roof of green.

Ganwar says that the farm will
have its new owner at the end of summer.
Lou can stay till fall,
and then they will tear down the buildings.
Lou is sad, he says.
She misses me.

I say he can tell Lou and Gol
that I miss them.
But I will not be coming back.

Hannah tries to take my mind off the farm.
She knows all the secret summer things.
We take the bus to a swimming hole
shaped like a giant brick.
It's filled with blue water and
laughing children.
First hot sun is on your skin,
then you jump in!
For a while,
you are a fish
in a warm, pretending lake.

She takes me to the library, too,
like the one at school,

only with enough books
for the whole world to read.
They give me a card with my name on it,
and let me look at book after book.
The library workers don't even know me,
and yet they promise I can take books home.
To be trusted with such precious gifts
is a great honor.
My father would have sung me
a song of pride
to see his son so trusted.

Hannah helps me find books
with pictures of Africa.
They don't seem real, these flat colors
smooth to my fingers. They make me
happy but also sad.
I see a picture of a woman,
tall with strong arms and sunny eyes,
and for a moment,
a crazy moment,
I think it might be my mother.

She's like her,
I say to Hannah.

But not.

She's very beautiful, Hannah says.

I'm starting to not remember,
I whisper. Sometimes I can't
see her face in my mind.
Only when I'm asleep now
is she real.

I know, Hannah says.
It's the same for me, too.
The words steal her smile away,
like clouds over sun.

On the library table is paper
in little pieces in a box,
and a cup filled with short yellow pencils.
I give a pencil to Hannah.

You can still send a letter to her, I say.
I wait. She doesn't speak.
I say, You can, but
I cannot.

Hannah lets air out slowly
from her mouth.
She looks at me with her
leave-me-alone face.
But she takes the pencil.

It's a very small paper, I say.
It can be a very short letter.

She chews on the pencil.
She twirls hair around her finger.
She makes another face at me.

But when she starts to write,
she can't stop.
She fills paper after paper
with words.

At last she's done.
There, she says.
Happy?

I smile. Yes.
Now we'll go mail it.

Fine. She makes another
sighing noise.
And then I'll whip your butt
at basketball.

I don't mind that so much.
She's mad, but it's a
good kind of mad.
Besides, she always
beats me at basketball.

MORE BAD NEWS

One hot day, Dave comes by to see how we are doing.
Hannah and I are in the parking lot.
She's teaching me how to skateboard.
I have many hard places on my knees and elbows
and a hat like a round ball on my head.
This is good because I fall down every time
I try to stand on the skateboard.
Hannah is trying not to laugh.
I am trying not to fall.

Lookin' good, buddy, Dave says,
but he is just being kind.
Why don't you take a break for a minute?
I've got some things to talk over with you.
I talked to Lou yesterday.

We sit on a bench in front of the apartment.
Hannah comes, too.

So you know about the farm, I say.
I take off my round extra head
and give it to Hannah.

I'm sorry, Dave says. I know you
liked working there.
I'll try to find you another place to help out.

Another place won't have Gol, I say.

Listen, buddy, Dave says,
I'm afraid I've got some more news.
I heard from Diane.
They tracked down the people who made it
to the two refugee camps we told you about.

Something grabs my throat
and tries to steal the air away.

None of them was your mom, Kek.

I look away.
Nearby a crow flaps his great, black wings
to chase away a sparrow.
Hannah pats my back.
There's still hope, though,
right? she asks.

Dave clears his throat.
There's another small refugee camp
about eighty miles south.
We're checking out that one.

I nod.

Remember how your aunt told me
you're an optimist, Kek? Dave asks.
I need you to stay strong.

In my pocket I feel the soft blue and yellow
fabric I have carried for so long.
I remember something Ganwar said to me.

Thank you for your helping, Dave, I say,
but what I'm thinking
is that a man knows when he's defeated.

SLEEP STORY

I'm in our tent at the camp,
and all around me children and women sleep.
We are too crowded to lie down.
We sleep on each other, legs and arms twined.
There is moaning and snoring and muttering and drooling,
but it's a kind of uneasy peace.
I'm not so hungry tonight.
Grain came in bags from the helping people today.

Mosquitoes buzz at the tent flaps,
louder and louder still,
and then I know it is the drone of a flying boat.
The gunfire is almost gentle at first—pop—pop—pop,
and then it gets closer
and the world goes crazy with fear.

Children scream, mothers sob, men threaten.
A fire is burning somewhere close.
My mother takes my hand, firm, sure.
Come, my child, she says, as if we are

going for a walk to look at the moon.
We run from the tent
pretending a safe place lies just a few steps away.
My mother falls, her dress caught on a bush,
and then the gunfire comes harder,
flying toward us like hot little stars.
Run, Kek, my mother screams, run now.
I kneel beside her. I can't leave you, I say,
or I think I say, for my voice is swallowed
by the roaring night.
My leg's hurt, I can't run. You hide in the trees.
You can get help for me when it's safe.
Go. Now.

I start to run and I don't know
that I'm clutching her dress
and a tiny piece rips free
and I run
and the trees are waiting
and the men come
with their knives and their guns and their mysterious hate.

I wait with other children.
I hold a little child and cover her mouth

when she tries to cry.
Dawn comes, silence comes,
blood and death are everywhere.

And my mother is gone.

CONFESSION

I awake to no blood, no bodies,
no Mama.
I'm on the sofa, and Ganwar sits on the floor
next to me.

You were moaning, he says.
It must have been a bad one.

I wipe my wet cheeks.
Very bad. I was in the camp,
and the men with guns came.

Ganwar nods. He clicks on a light
and the shadows take form.
I still have that one sometimes.

Not like this one. I shiver.

How can you be so sure? he asks.
You can't visit my head.

Because mine has truth in it, I say.
Because in mine—
I drop my head in my hands—
because in mine I leave Mama
and run.
In mine I'm a coward.
And it's the truth.

Ganwar stares past me for a long time.
He is somewhere far away
and I know where it is.
We all ran, Kek.
It's the only reason we're here.

I should have stayed with her.

Even a brave man can't stop a bullet.
You did what you had to do.

Ganwar joins me on the sofa.
He puts his arm around me.

He doesn't seem surprised
when I begin to sob.

And I'm not so surprised
when he, too, begins to cry.

RUNNING AWAY

I wait till Ganwar falls asleep.
I don't want to be here anymore.
I don't want to be in a place where
my words taste wrong in my mouth.
I don't want to live in a place where
candy for a kind girl makes people angry
and every year the trees must die.

I want to be in a place where the things
I love and know
are there within my reach.
But where is that place?

My aunt says I can find sun
when the sky is dark.
But she's wrong.
I can't see what isn't there.

I check the jar where I keep my pay from Lou.
I have a handful of green papers
and four silver washing machine coins.
With such riches I can run far away

to places I've seen on the TV machine,
although it will mean a lot of walking.
Maybe I can go to Washington
to the President's house,
and ask him to help find Mama.

I know two buses—
the bus to the grocery store and the mall,
and the one to Lou's farm.
I will take the bus that comes
to the bus stop first,
and then at least I will be on my way.

I would like to leave a note
so that my aunt and Ganwar and Hannah
won't worry about me.
But I don't know yet how to write many words.

Ganwar snores softly.
I leave half the green papers on the sofa.
I write my name on a scrap of paper.
I make a heart shape like the one I gave Hannah.
I get my jacket.
And I go.

BUS

The evening air is cool and damp.
I take the first bus that comes—
the route that goes past Lou's.
I put my coins in the hungry metal mouth
beside the driver.
The bus jerks and I grab a pole.
How far does this bus go? I ask.

To the airport, he says.

The airport? I repeat.
With the flying boats?

The driver gives me a strange look.
Sit down, kid.

I think about this important news
as I take a seat.
For the first time
I wonder if I could go back home.
I have my green money papers, after all.

I could fly to my home
and find my mother myself.
That is what a good son would do.

I think of the vastness
of my country.
I think of the camp,
the guns, the blood.
I wonder if flying back home
would be like the time I tried to fly
from the top of the acacia tree.

The bus is nearly empty.
We pass many buildings
and take many turns,
and then we are on a big street I know well.

In the soft light I see familiar places:
the gas stations,
the empty lots,
the cars for sale
with bright lights on a string overhead
like captured stars.

This is an ugly land, I think.
It needs endless horizons and
emptiness.
Here, too many buildings block the sky.
You can't even watch the sun
put on his bright pajamas
and sink into bed.

We're coming close to Lou's.
I feel bad not to have said
my thank-yous and good-byes
and to have shouted at Lou in anger.
In my old home,
where death sneaks into your home
in the hush of night,
good-byes were a precious thing.

How can I miss a place of such pain? I wonder.
It doesn't make sense.
And yet there it is.
What I miss
is the time before the pain.
I miss Mama and Lual and
listening to my father sing
a laughing song.

In the moonlight, I see first the old gray fence,
with new boards on the gate
Ganwar and I had fixed.
I see Lou's house,
the tree with its great brown arms outstretched,
the sagging barn.

I see Gol, too.
She is in the field alone,
staring out at the road.
I touch the window.
And then,
I don't know why,
I yell for the driver to stop.

TREED

By the time I'm over the fence,
Gol has spotted me.
She trudges over,
slow but determined,
like an old woman
longing for her grandchild's embrace.
When we reach each other,
I put my head on her neck.

You should be in the barn, I say.
I peer over her to see if Lou is outside.
The sky is rich with stars,
like fresh black dirt
sprinkled with tiny seeds.
The moon hangs low,
a cupped hand of silver water.

Gol nudges me.
I know this means she wants an ear scratch
so I do as I am told.
Tears warm my cheeks.

A door slams.
I see Lou heading to the barn.
I crouch low beside Gol.
I don't want Lou to see me crying.

She will be coming to get Gol,
and I must hide.
The field is empty. There's nowhere
to go but the big tree.

I dash over and clamber up easily.
It's a good climbing tree.
High up in the tangle of branches,
I watch the cars charge by
like a herd of panicked animals.

Gol looks up at me,
wondering why her ear scratch is over.
She heads slowly in the direction of the tree.
I wipe my nose on my sleeve.
No, I say softly. Go away, Gol.

She settles in under the tree
and stares up at me like a
motherless puppy.

I'm so high,
I should be able to see forever.
In the starlight I imagine that
if I try hard enough,
I can see my family's thatched hut,
my father's sharp-horned cattle,
the tree where I learned
I'm not meant to be a bird.

Go away, I whisper.

I am going to be here for a long time.

GANWAR

I have been in the tree forever
when I hear a bus screech to a stop.
Far across the field
I can just make out a tall figure
climbing down the bus stairs.
Ganwar leaps over the fence
and strides across the field.

He's heading toward the barn,
but then he stops. He looks at Gol.
He looks up into the branches of my tree.
And he laughs.

Please don't tell me
you're trying to fly again, he says.

How did you find me here? I ask in a loud whisper.

I woke up when you shut the door.
I watched from the window when you got on the bus
and I took the next one.

Why? I demand.

Ganwar shrugs. Don't know exactly.
But it was worth it, just to see you
stuck up there.

Using his good hand,
in one graceful move
he climbs up to join me.

I don't want company, I say.

He ignores me. So you're running away?

I'm *trying*.

Where to?

Maybe I am going home to find Mama.

Ganwar nods. You think that's what she would want?

It's what a man would do, I say.

Ganwar rubs his chin. Hmmm. What if she's
already on her way here?

I rub my eyes. Suddenly I feel tired.
If I lie back on this branch, I feel I could
fall asleep for a week.
I'm not used to making so many decisions.
I'm not used to so many changes.
In my old world, I was just Kek,
the silly boy. I was Lual's little brother,
Ganwar's troublesome cousin,
my parents' mischievous child.
That was all,
and that was enough.

I sigh. There are too many hard things,
I say softly. I can barely hear my own words.
It isn't fair.
I just want . . . I want everything I lost.

Ganwar rubs the place where his hand should be.
I look away.
I don't want to think about what
he has lost.
Maybe I'll come with you, Ganwar says.

No, I say firmly. You stay.

But it will never be right for me here, Kek.
I have this—he holds up his stump of an arm—
and I have the *gaar*. It's worse for me.
I'll never fit in.
If you're giving up,
why shouldn't I?

I don't answer him.
But when I look at Ganwar's arm,
I think of how he leapt into the tree
like it was his only home.
And how he does all the work I do
with just one good hand to help him.

I remember something my mama
used to say on dark days:
If you can talk, you can sing.
If you can walk, you can dance.

Ganwar, I whisper,
what if she never comes?

What if it's only . . . me?
I can't do it all by myself.

Ganwar sends me a sad smile.
My cousin, he says,
you already are.

TALK

I hear the crunch of someone walking.
Lou comes out of the barn.
Gol? she calls.
What are you up to, old girl?

Slowly Lou makes her way over.
She follows Gol's gaze up into the tree.
My, my, she says.
This may be the first time in history
a cow has treed two boys.

We climb down slowly.
When I get to the bottom,
Gol nudges me again.
She wants her ear scratch to continue.

I force myself to meet Lou's eyes.
Moonlight glints on her silver hair
like ice on snow.
I'm sorry, I say.
For being angry with you.

It isn't your fault
about the farm.

Lou smiles. Come on, you two.
I could use a hand.

We head toward the barn.
Gol follows.
Kind yellow light spills from the house.
Lou and Ganwar and I stand there in the silent barn,
stroking Gol
and waiting.

After a while, I help Lou
toss some fresh hay into Gol's stall.
How'd you end up in my tree this evening?
Lou finally asks.

I don't want to say the truth.
But when Lou looks right at you, you cannot
make up stories.
I'm running away, I say.

I see.
Lou thinks about this for a moment.
Want a cookie before you go?

I think, too.
A cookie would not be such a bad thing.

Chocolate? I ask.

Yep.

I follow Lou and Ganwar into the house.
It might be a long time
before I see chocolate again.

CHANGES

I take a handful of cookies
to show my gratitude.
Lou sits across from us at the
kitchen table.
The light spreads gentle shadows.

So you're running away,
Lou says. That's a mighty big job.

I watch while Lou gets us glasses of milk.
On top of the cold box there is a picture in a frame.
I see a pretty woman smiling.
A man has his arm around her.
He is tall and proud.
Behind the woman is a small tree.

Lou follows my gaze.
That's me, she says. A very long time ago.
And my husband, Robert. And that tree
is the one you two climbed just now.

I stare at the picture, then back at Lou.
If I try very hard and think *once upon a time,*
I think maybe I can find that young woman in her face.

I imagine a time when the barn didn't sag
and the cattle were many and strong
and hope grew fast
as flowers in good earth.
I imagine Lou saying good-bye soon to this place
that has been her home for so long,
to live in a world with no snow and no cows.

Lou pulls down another picture.
This is my sister, the one in L.A., she says.
She has a little yard.
I suppose I could plant some
vegetables there. You can grow things year round.
She stares at the picture.
Imagine that.

I spot a tiny seed of something fine sprouting
in Lou's eyes.
My heart is glad to see it.

I remember my aunt's words:
Kek finds sun when the sky is dark.
That was easy to do when I was a child
in my life before.
It's not so easy when the clouds are low and black.

I wonder if finding the sun is one way to be a man.

I drink my milk.
The clock ticks.
Ganwar and Lou are watching me.

I know it would be better to wait for Mama here,
I say at last.

Lou and Ganwar nod.
They don't say anything.

I guess I could come back to work
until you have to leave, I add.

That would be great, Lou says.
I know Gol would like that.

She could use more attention,
Ganwar says.

That cow does love a good ear scratch,
Lou agrees.

She's good for petting, I say.

And leaning on, Ganwar adds.

She's a very unusual cow, Lou says.

Another idea comes into my head
like a new friend knocking at the door.
Sometimes I very much like my brain, I say.

What do you mean? Ganwar asks.

I smile. I think maybe I just found
some sun for Gol.

PART FOUR

When spider webs unite,
they can tie up a lion.
—AFRICAN PROVERB

HERDING

When Saturday comes,
Lou is waiting for
Ganwar and Hannah and me
in the barn.

She sips at her coffee mug.
I just wish my trailer hitch
hadn't rusted out, she says.

We'll be fine, I tell her.

Hannah is wearing her school backpack.
I brought a map in case we get lost, she says.
And some candy bars and water.

It's a long way, Lou says in a worried voice.
There's a lot of traffic.

She shakes her head.
I probably shouldn't be letting you do this.

You probably don't have a choice,
Ganwar says with a laugh.

Maybe I should call ahead
and explain things? Lou asks.

Sometimes it's better
just to walk up to the door
and ask, I say.

Lou grins. All right, then.
Let's get this show on the road.
She gives Gol a kiss.
See ya, girl.
It's been a good ride.

I take Gol's halter
and off we go.
The sun is a steady hand on our shoulders.

We walk along the side of the busy road
for many steps.

Gol and me,
then Hannah behind us,
then Ganwar.
When cars race by,
they suck the air away.

A huge truck grumbles past.
Gol doesn't like the whoosh and roar.
She stops hard
and refuses to go on.
I pull.
She pulls back.

She hates
being so close to the traffic, I say.

I pat Gol and talk to her
and after a while she
agrees to move on.
Good girl, I say, relieved.

But up ahead I see trouble is waiting.

TRAFFIC JAM

We reach a crossing of two huge roads.
Many lights hang from wires.
Cars come and go
like frantic ants.

Don't worry, Ganwar says.
I'll tell you when it's safe.
He turns to Hannah.
You sure this is the right way?

Pretty sure, she answers.

Ganwar watches the lights,
then steps into the road.
A blue car zooms toward him,
horn blaring.

He leaps back.
We wait a while longer,
then Ganwar dives back into the traffic.
Come on. He waves his hand.
And hurry!

We cross three lanes of cars
and come to a thin strip of land
covered with grass and tiny purple flowers.
We've still got three more lanes, Ganwar says.

But Gol has decided
the purple flowers are a tasty treat.
She grazes happily
while I yank on her harness.
Hannah pushes Gol's rump.
Come on, girl! Ganwar cries.

The light turns yellow.
Hurry! Hannah yells.

Gol glances up
to see what all the noise is about.
She chomps down one last bite.
Then she ambles out into the road.

The light turns red.
We are in the middle of a sea of cars.
Honking and shouting hurts our ears.
Gol looks at me

as if to say,
Why is everyone in such a hurry?

I pull, Hannah and Ganwar push.
And nobody moves.

Gol has come to a stop,
and so has all the traffic.

COPS

We are surrounded by cars,
but no one is moving.
It looks like the parking lot at the mall.
Only everyone is grouchy.

If you don't get that cow off the road,
she's gonna be lunch meat, kid! a man screams.

Look, Mommy!
A little girl points out her window.
Is this a parade?

Heading slowly toward us
I see bright lights of red, white and blue.
Great, Ganwar mutters.
Cops.

The car with lights gets stuck in traffic, too.
A woman and a man in blue soldier clothes
make their way through the knot of cars.
They have guns on their hips.

What's going on here, kids?
the policewoman asks.

My cow won't move, I explain.
It's hard to take my eyes off
her gun.

Some reason your cow is in the
middle of six lanes of traffic
on a busy Saturday? the policeman asks.

We're going to the zoo, Hannah says.
Ganwar covers his eyes and groans.

The police people can't decide
whether to smile or frown.
Their mouths are all mixed up.

You taking her to see the animals
or *be* one of the animals?
the woman asks.

Hannah clears her throat.
Um, she's going to be
a new exhibit.

Who's going to pay to see this
bag of bones? the man asks.

She's going to be in the petting zoo,
I explain. She likes to have her ears scratched.
Go on. Try it.

Not me. The policeman holds up his hands.
I wanna get close to one of these,
I'll get a Value Meal with fries.

The policewoman holds out her hand and
reaches for Gol's ear.
Gol leans into her.
She likes me, the woman says.

Horns blare.
Uh, Nora, we got to focus here,
the policeman says.

She might move now,
I say. We'll push, and maybe
you can pull.

This is definitely not part of my
job description, the man mutters.

We get into position.
One, two, three!
Ganwar cries. Move!

Gol looks behind her.
She's pouting a little.
She can see she is surrounded.
Slowly she inches forward.

Bit by bit,
we cross the rest of the road.

Cars begin to move again.
Some people who drive by
use words I haven't learned
in ESL class yet.

It's very dangerous for you kids
to be doing this, the woman says
when we reach the other side.
Why isn't she in a trailer or something?
Who owns this cow, anyway?

Lou gave me custard, I say proudly.

The police just stare.

Custody, I correct myself.
I pull out the piece of paper
Lou gave me.

The man examines the paper.
He sighs. Well, it's just a few more miles up the road.
I suppose we could give you an escort.

I don't know what this is,
but I can tell that Hannah is excited.
Would you keep your lights on? she asks.

Lights, but no siren, the woman agrees.

We begin our slow, strange herding down the
edge of the highway,
followed by the police car.
The red, white and blue lights

remind me of the America flag.
I feel like the President.

If only Lual could be here,
I say to Ganwar,
and we laugh a good, long laugh.

ZOO

The zoo workers are a little surprised
to see one cow, three kids and a police car
show up at the ticket booth.
They call their bosses
and say come quick.
The zoo bosses are even more surprised
when I tell them Lou and I
are donating Gol
to the petting zoo.

Just try scratching her ear, I say.

She loves it, adds the policewoman.

The main zoo boss is
tall and thin and has
a shiny head like an apple
at the grocery store.

He reaches out for Gol's right ear.
Gol makes her happy cow face.
Her eyes are faraway and full of peaceful thoughts.

You are a charmer, aren't you, old girl?
says the man.

The petting zoo needs a cow, Hannah points out.

And she is free, Ganwar adds.
The owner is donating her,
even though she could sell her
and make a fine profit.

Everyone looks at Ganwar.
He shrugs. Figured it was worth a try, he says.

This is a very kind offer,
says another zoo boss man.
but this isn't how we do things usually, kids.
There are meetings, and requisition forms,
and veterinary exams—

Gol rests her head on the
shoulder of the apple-head zoo boss.
I can see that she is very tired from
her adventure today.

She's awfully affectionate, Harold,
the man says. And they make a point.
We *are* in need of a cow.

I was hoping for one a little less . . .
geriatric, Harold replies.

Gol blinks her long-lashed eyes
and Harold smiles.
Oh, what the heck, he says,
and once again I see that
heck is a very good word.
Why don't we send her over to the clinic
and have her checked out?
If she's clean and in decent health . . .
well, she does kind of grow on you.

Ganwar leans close to me.
You amaze me, cousin.

Hannah kisses Gol
and Ganwar pats her flank
and I stroke her neck
and whisper in her ear
and then off she goes

to her new land
to begin again.

The police drive us home in their car.
They keep the lights on
and even play the siren once.

What did you whisper to Gol?
Hannah asks when we return to Lou's.

I grin.
I told her if she can moo,
she can sing.

EPILOGUE

FIFTEEN MONTHS LATER

A sandstorm passes;
the stars remain.
—*AFRICAN PROVERB*

HOMECOMING

The airplanes float in
one by one
but each one is the wrong one
and we wait
and wait
and wait some more.

Ganwar and his new girlfriend
and Dave and my aunt
sit on the plastic chairs
and talk.

Hannah stands beside me
as we stare out the wall of glass.
We know enough to be quiet.

In the pocket of Hannah's jeans
I see part of a white envelope

covered in curly blue letters.
I smile.
Hannah carries it with her everywhere.
I know how that is.

It's fall,
and the trees are wearing red and orange coats
to fight the icy nights.
I think about the trees, the flowers,
the brown grass in the fields.
They can all be patient,
certain that spring will return.
They don't have to hope.
They can be sure.

Hope is a thing made only for people,
a scrap to hold onto
in darkness and in light.

But hope is hard work.
When I was a child, I hoped to fly.
That was a silly, easy wish.
Now my wishes are bigger,
the hopes of a man,
and they take much tending,

like seedlings in rough sun.
Now I hope to make my new life work,
to root to this good, hard land
forever.

At last the time comes
and the door opens
and people pour out
but no one
is the right one.

The sun streams through the glass window.
red and gold with the day's last sighs,
so bright I have to shade my eyes.
One more person comes out,
slow and searching.
I see other colors, too, then,
blue and yellow,
not the colors of the setting sun,
but a flash of something torn from my past.

A voice comes,
a voice like laughing water
on my thirsty heart:
My son!

and Mama embraces me
like we're saying good-bye
instead of hello
and around her neck is a scarf
made of the softest fabric
of blue and yellow.

I can't find words.
There are no words, not in my old language,
not in my new one.
We walk together
like one person,
her arm tight around my shoulders,
and the air is wild with talking and
laughter and questions,
so many questions,
but I don't speak.

We reach the silver escalator
with its melting stairs.
Mama freezes.
People grumble
and step around her.

I take a breath,
I take a step,
I hold out my hand.
She watches me rise,
she takes my hand
and at last
the right words come.

Mama, I say,
welcome home.

Thank you for reading this FEIWEL AND FRIENDS book.

The FRIENDS who made *Home of the Brave* possible are:

JEAN FEIWEL, *Publisher*

LIZ SZABLA, *Editor-in-Chief*

RICH DEAS, *Creative Director*

ELIZABETH FITHIAN, *Marketing Director*

ELIZABETH USURIELLO, *Assistant to the Publisher*

DAVE BARRETT, *Managing Editor*

NICOLE LIEBOWITZ MOULAISON, *Production Manager*

Find out more about our authors and artists
and our future publishing at
WWW.FEIWELANDFRIENDS.COM

Our Books are Friends for Life